*Hi, Josephine,*

A BOTANIC HILL DETECTI

MW00878193

# NUTMEG STREET:

# EGYPTIAN SECRETS

*Reading makes you smarter. Read every day!*

BY

## SHERRILL JOSEPH

♡ *Sherrill Joseph*

*7/17/21*

FROM THE TINY ACORN...
GROWS THE MIGHTY OAK

Nutmeg Street: Egyptian Secrets. First Edition
Copyright © 2020 Sherrill M. Joseph. All rights reserved.
Printed in the United States of America. For information, address
Acorn Publishing, LLC, 3943 Irvine Blvd. Ste. 218, Irvine, CA 92602

www.acornpublishingllc.com

Cover design by eBook Launch

Digital Formatting and Interior Design by Debra Cranfield Kennedy

Map of Botanic Hill by Hayley Lekven

Library of Congress Control Number: 2019910950

ISBN: 978-1-947392-58-8

To all my students from thirty-five years of teaching
In the San Diego Unified School District.
You taught me more than I could ever teach you.
I am honored to have been your teacher.

AND

To Connie Colonelli deWerd, aka, "Miss Colonelli,"
My favorite teacher, mentor, and lifelong friend.
In second grade, you taught me heady words like *igneous,*
*Sedimentary, metamorphic, sarcophagus,* and *Tutankhamun.*
Your beauty, cool clothes, and sports cars
Were legendary at school.
Add those amazing art projects, innovative learning activities,
And exotic travel slides, and you lit up my childhood.
Because of you, I eventually had students and sport cars,
But my French twist hairdo was no match for yours.
Now, an Egyptian mystery.
You still inspire my journey.

HE WHO COMMITS INJUSTICE
IS EVER MORE WRETCHED
THAN HE WHO SUFFERS IT.

PLATO, GREEK PHILOSOPHER
428 B.C.E.–348 B.C.E.

# CONTENTS

# NUTMEG STREET:
## EGYPTIAN SECRETS

# THE BEAUTIFUL NEIGHBORHOOD
## OF BOTANIC HILL

The views from every street in the charming neighborhood
of Botanic Hill are spectacular. Looking west, our four
detectives can see the vast turquoise Pacific Ocean as it
crashes ashore in their resort town of Las Palmitas. Due
east, snow glistens from the rolling Laguna Mountains in
the otherwise mild Southern California winters. Hidden are
the beautiful Anza-Borrego Desert and the agriculturally
rich region of the Imperial Valley, stretching toward
Arizona and Baja California.

Long ago for Botanic Hill, city planners mapped out
twenty-six streets from A to Z, running east-west, in honor
of the area's impressive array of botanicals. Most
everything grows here.

Dear Reader, may you have fun exploring and solving
mysteries with our detectives—twins Lanny and Lexi
Wyatt, Moki Kalani, and Rani Kumar—from Acacia Street
on the hill's southern border, to Zinnia Street in the north,
and on all the streets in between. Each is a riot of lush trees
and fragrant blossoms. But be careful! Danger often lurks
in Paradise.

# Map of Botanic Hill

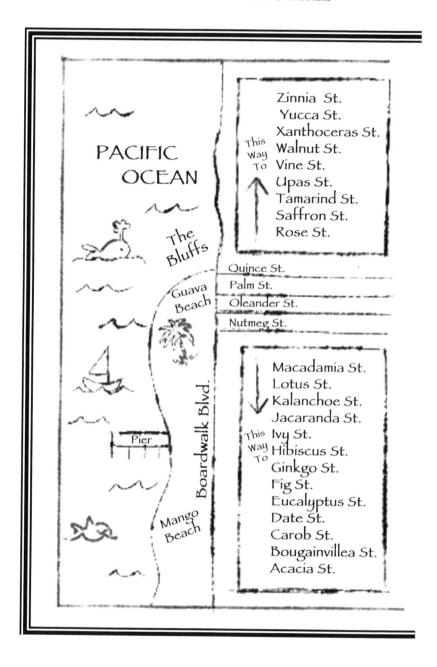

PACIFIC OCEAN

The Bluffs

Guava Beach

Pier

Boardwalk Blvd.

Mango Beach

This Way To ↑
Zinnia St.
Yucca St.
Xanthoceras St.
Walnut St.
Vine St.
Upas St.
Tamarind St.
Saffron St.
Rose St.

Quince St.
Palm St.
Oleander St.
Nutmeg St.

↓ Macadamia St.
Lotus St.
Kalanchoe St.
Jacaranda St.
This Way To Ivy St.
Hibiscus St.
Ginkgo St.
Fig St.
Eucalyptus St.
Date St.
Carob St.
Bougainvillea St.
Acacia St.

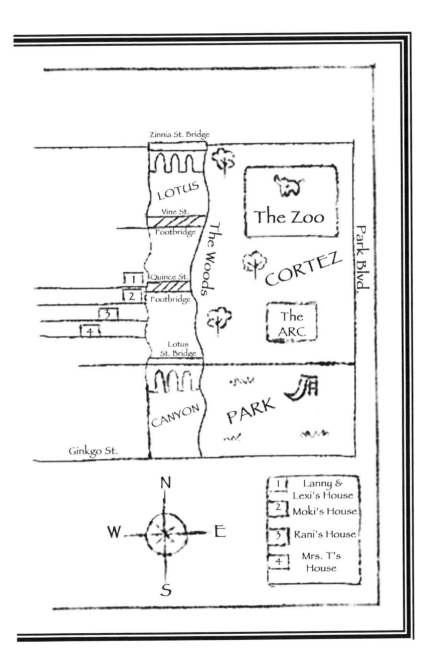

# CHAPTER ONE

· ✧ ·

# A Mystery from Nutmeg Street

Dead eyes, with years of curses and murder in them, stared back at thirteen-year-old Lexi Wyatt. She smiled. Lexi loved a good mummy and anything Egyptian. And a gripping mystery.

She and her friends treated Dr. Thornsley's musty study like a shrine, with all its carefully copied treasures from Dr. T's many Egyptian expeditions. She turned from the mummy mask on the wall to question Mrs. Thornsley but saw her twin brother, Lanny, walking toward her. He had a look Lexi knew meant her blond, brainiac brother wanted to share an important thought. Which meant he shared all his thoughts, Lexi decided, since he always had that look and considered everything he thought important.

"Lexi," he whispered, "I just realized something. You and I are like ancient Egyptian kings and queens!"

She hesitated a moment, trying to decide if hearing his explanation was worth letting Lanny have his ego moment. Yes, she decided—if she was like Egyptian royalty, she wanted to know why. "Okay, I give. Explain."

"Well," he started, "Dad is a famous archaeologist, and Mom is an equally famous art historian, right? And because of them, we get access to all kinds of amazing places and people and adventures, right? We benefit from our lineage, just like princes and princesses do when they become queens and kings. See? Kings and queens—us! It's all about lineage."

"Oh," she said. "Good one." She could stand being like any royalty, but especially Egyptian.

And it wasn't all that big a stretch, really. They did get to accompany their parents on many business trips around the world for the Antiquities Research Collective—or the ARC, as everyone in town called the "think tank" in beautiful Cortez Park. Not only did the twins' parents work there, but so had Dr. Thornsley. Lexi dreamed of imitating the kind, brilliant man by becoming an Egyptologist herself someday. Then, she would work at the ARC as a vital member of the team of some of the world's most renowned archaeologists and art historians.

Lanny and Lexi's best friends, Moki Kalani and Rani Kumar, often went along on the ARC-sponsored adventures. Best of all, somehow, all their experiences with fascinating people and places ended up with them finding some mystery or other. They'd even started calling themselves detectives, looking for cases to solve. It was the best life Lexi could imagine. Those were the reasons the Wyatt twins, plus Moki and Rani, were here today, in the study of Dr. and Mrs. Thornsley's big old house on Nutmeg Street. They were about to hear their first real mystery.

But this mystery hit home because their family friend, the extraordinary Egyptologist, Dr. Thornsley, was dead.

Lexi returned to her task, addressing Mrs. Thornsley. "So you say, Mrs. T, four months ago Dr. T started getting mysterious phone calls." Lexi gently ran her finger over a stubby pencil that had been used by Dr. Thornsley, whom she would never forget. "He'd jump up and lock the study door after saying hello. Sometimes, his voice would rise in anger, and then he'd bang down the landline receiver. Have I got that right?"

"Yes, that's right, Alexia. The calls started last February right after Dr. Thornsley and I returned from a short trip out of town." Mrs. Thornsley fidgeted with the old, curly telephone cord. "He changed the subject whenever I mentioned the calls, but I . . . I think he was being threatened."

Lexi set her hand on the widow's shoulder, looking fondly at the kind, fashionably dressed woman who often called her "Alexia" rather than her nickname. "Don't worry, Mrs. T. We'll find out what's going on."

Being smart and confident, they knew they would. Just last year when they were in France with the twins' parents, they inadvertently helped the French police catch two jewel thieves and a sizable hoard of diamond bracelets stolen from a Paris jewelry store. The crooks crashed right into the four kids, who were strolling past the expensive shop. The gemstones went flying out of the thieves' pockets and onto the sidewalk in plain sight of many pedestrians. That lucky accident led to the police uncovering a ring of international jewel thieves. The news and photos went viral. After returning home to a citywide celebration in their honor, the squad officially established their Botanic Hill Detectives Agency.

But this case was right in their neighborhood. They had to solve it, mainly for Dr. and Mrs. Thornsley.

Thirteen-year-old Rani gracefully pivoted to face Mrs. Thornsley, her gold and turquoise sari twirling just a bit. Whenever possible, she preferred wearing clothing from her native country of India. She knew that girls' saris were usually reserved for festivals, but she loved honoring her culture. Besides, her dear grandmother made them for her. "You said something else happened here in the study, Mrs. T?" She drew a squiggle on the dusty top of Dr. Thornsley's wooden desk.

"Actually, two more strange occurrences, Rani. Three months ago, in March, an old framed picture from this very desk went missing." Mrs. T's index finger jabbed decisively at its surface. "It showed Dr. Thornsley twenty years ago with some people I never knew from his hometown back East. When I asked him what had happened to it, he said the picture had fallen from the desk and broken. He had planned to get a new frame, but the picture never reappeared.

One month later . . . he died." Mrs. Thornsley covered her face with her hands. She worked hard to choke back some sobs. Rani came to her side and put her arm around the woman.

After a moment, she continued. "Then one afternoon last month, I came home from running errands to discover that someone had broken into this room. Nothing appeared to be missing, but this desk had been ransacked. The police found no fingerprints or other clues to lead them to a suspect." Mrs. Thornsley could no longer control herself. Tears flooded down the furrows in her face. She fretfully wrung her tired, wrinkled hands. Lexi, always emotional, teared up, too.

Seeing the two crying, Moki looked around and nervously shifted his weight from one foot to the next. "Hey, uh, Mrs. T," he asked, "what's that I see over there on the coffee table?" The Hawaiian boy, who had moved to Southern California five years ago, pointed beyond the study door. With big eyes, Lanny silently thanked Moki for the rescue.

"Bless you, Moki," said the woman. "You read my mind. I've had enough of this room for a while. Let's go. I set out some snacks for you four in the living room. It's been very difficult for me to spend any time in this study alone, you know, since my husband's death in April." Mrs. Thornsley dabbed at her eyes with a tissue and squeezed Rani's small but strong hand.

"That makes perfect sense to me, Mrs. T," replied Lexi,

blinking back a tear while supporting Mrs. Thornsley with an arm around the woman's small waist. The girl snapped off the wall switch to the study's overhead light fixture with her free hand.

Moki, a confirmed foodie, bounded into the living room. His Hawaiian shirt was a blur of colors as he ran and barely missed clipping his side on the woman's enormous grand piano. His huge brown eyes had zeroed in on a platter piled high with cookies.

Mrs. Thornsley couldn't resist a booming laugh. "Oh, Moki. You're like medicine for my poor, sad soul. Please, do help yourself. You've earned your fill."

"Thanks. Don't mind if I do." He lunged toward the platter and dug into the cookies. "Mmm, chocolate chip," Moki said through a mouthful. "My fave."

Lexi and Rani served everyone some of the frosty lemonade from the nearby crystal pitcher.

They stared as Moki grabbed a third large cookie. "Oinkers!" snorted Lexi.

"Huh?" he replied with crumbs cascading from his lips.

"Didn't you have breakfast this morning?" asked Lexi.

"Sure, but that was almost two hours ago. Anyway, mysteries make me hungry," he croaked between chomps.

No one seemed to have noticed that Lanny had remained behind in Dr. Thornsley's study. Something had caught his eye. The room's lighting was subdued now, and the study was as still as a tomb. Lanny felt as if he had been transported back in time to ancient Egypt. Such was the magic of this room. The only movement came from some dust particles that danced inside a splinter of sunlight stealing in through the sheer-curtained French doors behind Dr. Thornsley's massive wooden desk.

A low cabinet beneath Lexi's favorite mummy mask contained, among other mementos, meticulously detailed, expensive copies of assorted treasures from Dr. T's excavations. There were miniature cat- and ibis-headed statues and raised cobras on pharaohs' headdresses. In addition, Dr. Thornsley had displayed his old compass, badly scratched by desert sands, yellowed dig-site maps, and various archaeological tools. Though fascinating, he and his friends had seen these objects before in what Lexi called Dr. T's mini museum during their frequent visits to Nutmeg Street.

What had actually grabbed Lanny's attention was an out-of-place object on the floor to the left of Dr. T's desk. He stooped to pick it up. It was a small sandstone sphinx. Its right forepaw had cracked off. Lanny knelt and rummaged under the desk and soon found the broken piece, reuniting it with the maimed original already cupped in his left hand.

From his low position on the floor, Lanny thought he saw a shadow cast on the rug. He turned around quickly to glance in the direction of the French doors. Nothing. It must have been his imagination. Or maybe Mrs. T's next-door neighbor was passing by in his side yard. Being a detective with a tendency toward curiosity, he decided to investigate.

Setting the pieces of the sphinx down on Dr. T's desk, he unlocked the doors and stepped outside into the mild breeze. Scanning the area, he saw no one and concluded the shadow could have been caused by some fluttering branches of the nearby weeping willow tree. He hesitated a moment, shrugged, and returned to the study, making certain to relock the doors. Then, he carefully picked up the sphinx pieces off the desk to show the others.

"Lanny, you better hurry before Moki eats all the cookies," Rani shouted over her shoulder just as the boy was rejoining the group. Cookie scents wafted to his nostrils, but he didn't have food on his mind.

Mrs. T's eyebrows knitted together as she stared at Lanny's hands. "What do you have there, Lanyon?" she asked. In answer, he put his palms face up to reveal his find.

"Oh, that was my husband's paperweight. He bought it in one of his favorite dusty, old curio shops in Giza on a trip to Egypt many years ago. It must have been too near the edge of his desk and gotten jostled off during the earthquake."

A moderate earthquake had, indeed, rumbled through their coastal resort town of Las Palmitas that very morning and snaked its way up into the group's beautiful neighborhood of Botanic Hill. They were all too familiar with earthquakes in Southern California.

"How he treasured that little sphinx so." She gently took the precious pieces from Lanny, cradling and inspecting them momentarily. "Fortunately, I think I can easily fix it."

Lanny watched the rest of the squad finish the snacks. He turned toward Mrs. Thornsley and said, "You said you called us here today to tell us about Dr. T's urn. Is it from the same expedition where he found the mummy mask that's on the wall in his study?"

"Yes, Lanyon, though the mask is just a copy of the original. My husband found both objects in Egypt at the royal burial grounds in Abydos last summer along with other treasures." The widow quickly pulled something from her pocket. "Here's a photo he took of the urn right after it arrived in his office at the ARC last October for study and display. He estimated the urn and mask to be 5,000 years old and priceless."

The kids crowded around the photo. "It's beautiful with all the golden swirling lotus designs on the black enamel paint," Lexi said. Her voice swelled with pride over Dr. Thornsley's discovery.

"And it contained a mummified Egyptian cobra," said Mrs. Thornsley with hiked-up eyebrows.

"Whoa!" Moki called out, abruptly removing his hand from the photo's edge. "Why would anyone want to keep a snake, even a dead one, in a jar?" He brushed his hands as if to remove something squirmy and toxic. Snakes didn't exist in his native Hawai'i. He was no fan of reptiles.

"It's a tomb burial urn, Moki, and snakes were sacred to ancient Egyptians," she replied.

"A 'sacred snake'? Sorry, but those words don't seem to go together in my head."

The woman paused. Her face had turned ashen again, but she slowly continued. "I realize you kids might already know some of this information, but you won't know all of it. After all, you've been busy solving other mysteries. You see, my husband was the last ARC employee to see the urn before it disappeared. The police couldn't find any other suspects, so he was blamed for stealing it. He died in shame from the rumors after a long and brilliant career. Oh, how I wish now he had never gone to Egypt last year to find that urn." She closed her eyes tightly to squeeze back any more tears and sighed. Silence engulfed the room.

Then, Mrs. Thornsley squared her slumped shoulders and went on. "Since law enforcement agencies seem to have hit a dead end in their investigations, I want to hire you four to find the urn and who really stole it, return the object to the ARC, and restore my husband's good name."

"Mrs. T, Lexi's right. We'll find out what's going on," Lanny replied. "In fact, we'll gladly take the case. But the theft occurred last fall. It's June now. Something must have happened recently to make you call us today. What was it?" He hesitated to question her. Would she dissolve in tears? Worse, would she call him "Lanyon" again? Moki delighted in teasing Lanny about his real name. But they needed to know why she had called.

"Yes, Lanyon, two things have happened. Dr. Abbott called me this morning and—"

But before the widow could continue, Rani gasped and pointed at the window. Mrs. Thornsley turned and uttered a little cry, drawing her hand up sharply to her mouth.

"What the heck!" Lexi shouted as she sprang to her feet.

Through the large front window, a face disguised by what resembled the death mask of an Egyptian pharaoh was gazing in at them. Sensing discovery, the trespasser immediately ducked away. The kids raced to the window in time to see someone squeeze back through the dense hydrangea bushes, rocket across the manicured lawn, and jump the hedge.

"The front door!" Lexi shouted, "Go, go, go!" She headed for the door with the two guys behind her. Rani was already there, yanking it open and bolting outside ahead of everyone.

"Teach that Mask Face a lesson," Moki hollered as he almost tripped over a footstool. "It's not nice to look in other people's windows."

"I'm with you, bro," Lanny replied. "Catch that nut!"

The four kids tore across Mrs. Thornsley's lawn and sprang over her low hedge in their hot pursuit of the brazen, masked trespasser. At the end of the block, they cut the corner sharply, not looking back to notice the broken branches and trampled flowers they left strewn down Nutmeg Street.

# CHAPTER TWO

· ✧ ·

# Helpful Discussions

Rani led the pack in the chase after the masked nut, her sari flapping behind her. After a few blocks, however, she was forced to stop. Her golden bangle bracelets glinted in the early afternoon sun as she wiped her brow with the back of her hand. Her friends soon caught up with her, panting for breath and unhappily conceding defeat. They hadn't been speedy enough to catch the trespasser, who had a good head start on them.

Several blocks away, they watched the wiry, still-disguised runner jump into the driver's seat of a parked blue sedan. The engine roared to life, and the car screeched down the street, leaving behind only thick tread marks.

"Whoever's behind that mask is really fit," said Rani, hunched over and sucking in oxygen.

Lexi bit her lower lip and narrowed her eyes. "That's a great clue, Rani. Let's hang onto it because it could help us identify the person. By the way, I'm impressed at how fast you can run in a sari."

Rani replied, "My grandmother would kill me if she knew. The fabric's very delicate. But more importantly, remind me to tell all of you later about mac 'n' cheese. It might be another clue."

"Huh? Mac 'n' cheese?" Moki asked. He always tuned in when food was mentioned. "What's that have to do with anything? Plus, you're making me hungry."

"I'll tell you later. Might help us with our case," she said with a mysterious smile, then sauntered back toward the house.

"Rani, sometimes I just don't get you," Moki called after her.

"Good. Mystery makes life interesting."

The four retraced their steps to the big Craftsman-style house, and Lanny shared their bad luck with Mrs. Thornsley. "Not even a license plate number," he said, jamming his knuckles into the palm of his hand with a loud pop. "I must be losing it."

"No, bro," Moki said, placing his hand on his best friend's shoulder. "They lost it—or more likely, someone removed it. No back license plate. But at least we have a description of the car and some info about the person and the tires. That'll be important to us and to the police." Moki would know. His dad was a cop.

Moki called the Las Palmitas Police Department to report the crime on Mrs. Thornsley's behalf. After hanging up he said, "According to the dispatcher, Dad's out on a call having to do with the earthquake, but some other officers will be here very soon. Now, no worries, Mrs. T."

The woman was pacing the floor like a caged tiger. "I just wish it was your dad coming instead. Oh, Moki, that's silly of me. I realize he's a busy man. It's just . . . why are burglars and trespassers so interested in my house all of a sudden?"

"We'll figure it out, Mrs. T," Lexi replied. She and Rani exchanged glances. They both knew how much serious work was ahead of them.

Two officers arrived just minutes after Moki's call, and Mrs. Thornsley breathed a sigh of relief. They took statements from all five witnesses about "Mask Face," as Moki named the trespasser, and checked the small footprints Rani had found in the soil outside under the living room window. Lanny mentioned the shadow he had seen through the study doors, but nothing appeared disturbed on the leaf-covered ground. The officers said a squad car would cruise past the Thornsley house several times an hour for the next two days. After checking all around the property one more time, the officers left to investigate the tire marks and to question the neighbors.

"Keep all your doors and windows locked, Mrs. Thornsley, and look out the spy hole before opening the door," one of the officers said gently.

"That's always good advice," the woman replied. "I'll certainly do as you say."

The kids wanted to make sure Mrs. Thornsley was feeling safe and composed before they left. "Don't worry, Mrs. T. We're on the job. We'll keep you posted on our progress," said Lanny. Lexi and Rani stood like bookends next to the woman.

Mrs. Thornsley led the kids to her huge front door, suddenly stopped, and gazed at the four kids. Her actions didn't go unnoticed.

"Is something wrong, Mrs. T?" asked Lanny.

"No, no, Lanyon. It's just . . . each of you has such a good vocabulary and seems very mature and polite for your thirteen years. Those are some of the reasons why I hired you."

Lanny replied, "Thanks. We've had lots of conversations with our parents about being professional. We take our detective agency work seriously." Lexi nodded.

"My parents expect me to be polite," Rani said.

"And my dad says there's no time like the present to practice responsibility," Moki added.

"Well, it's nice to see in your generation and makes me feel confident," Mrs. Thornsley said with a smile.

At the front door, she hugged each of them, waved good-bye, then lingered and watched them disappear up Nutmeg Street.

The squad was already mulling over their first case as the early afternoon sun warmed their faces. Finally, Rani said, "I don't think it was an accident that the trespasser wore an Egyptian death mask."

"Why do you say that?" Lanny asked, kicking a small stone off the sidewalk.

"It made an effective disguise, and an insensitive one at that, given what Mrs. T's already been through. Whoever was behind that mask could be the same person who ransacked Dr. T's study last month and returned today to continue the search."

Moki looked at Rani and replied, "That means, if I'm following your thinking for a change, that whatever was being searched for in the study last month is still being searched for."

"Exactly."

Lanny stopped walking. "Maybe, or it could have just been a mean prank. As my hero, the great fictional detective Sherlock Holmes, would say, 'Give me facts, not just suppositions.' We do need theories, you guys, but we can't suppose they're true until we have proof. Proof comes from facts. That's the scientific method of investigation, and so far, it's worked well for us."

Lanny was right. Boring, but right. Ever the voice of reason, an important quality in a detective. Each of the others had to admit it to themselves as they continued walking on in silence.

Soon, Moki disrupted the quiet. "Okay, so then, let's get serious and scientific now and talk about mac 'n' cheese. Rani, what's up with that, and how can it be a clue in our case?"

"It's simple. You see, I'm a synesthete," she replied brightly.

"A synes-what?" Moki asked. Even Lanny, always ready with a definition, looked puzzled.

"A synesthete. I have synesthesia," she said with a broad smile.

"Oh, now that clears everything up for me," he smirked. "Is it fatal?"

Rani grimaced. "Uh, no, Moki, but I'll explain. Synesthesia is a mixing of the senses, an extrasensory ability where one type of brain stimulation—let's say, hearing a word or name—makes you experience something else. In my case, that something else is a taste or smell. Isn't that cool?" She didn't wait for an answer.

"Well, anyway, some synesthetes associate a word, number, or musical note with a color. Those are the most common types. I associate words and names with foods or aromas. My type of synesthesia is very rare. Four percent of the world's population has some form of synesthesia. But less than one percent of the world's population has my type. Lots of famous people have had synesthesia. Van Gogh, Duke Ellington, Plato, and Socrates all had it."

"Wow!" Lexi said, then quickly frowned. "But we've been best friends for eight years. How come I'm only just learning this about you now?"

"I didn't know I had it, let alone that there was a name for it. I read an article about it online recently. Then it was as if a lightbulb flashed in me. 'Wow,' I thought, 'that's me!' I'd thought everybody associated names with food. I didn't know it was *a thing*."

"So synesthesia is an ability, not a disability?" Lanny asked looking steadily at the girl.

"Yes, and it's automatic. I can't turn it off, but I wouldn't want to. It makes life more, well, delicious. Plus, it helps me remember names. And it's like eating but without calories," she beamed.

"So, the moment of truth. What do our names make you taste or smell?" Moki asked.

"Oh, Moki, your name makes me taste warm blueberry pie with melting vanilla ice cream." She purposely emphasized the food words to make Moki hungry.

"Sweet. Of course," he replied with crossed arms and a knowing smile directed at Lexi.

"Lexi, you're crunchy, salty pretzels, the big heart-shaped kind. Lanny, you're sweet potatoes mashed with butter, salt, and pepper. And my name, Rani, is raw green beans."

"So, what's with mac 'n' cheese, and how can that help our case?" Moki asked.

"The word *mask* makes me taste mac 'n' cheese. It might be interesting to see if that sensation occurs again during our mystery," she replied.

They walked on to Rani's house one block away on Oleander Street, discussing other names and food associations. Once at Rani's, however, they knew they would turn to the serious business of hashing over their new case and formulating a plan of action for tomorrow.

✧

Lexi and Lanny didn't arrive home on Quince Street until the late afternoon. As they walked through the back door into the large, well-equipped kitchen, they were greeted by the spicy aromas of freshly chopped cilantro and cheesy homemade enchiladas, and by the family's cook and houseman, "Uncle" Rocky. He'd joined the family shortly before the twins were born. He had been the cook for one of Dr. Wyatt's archaeological excavations, and the two men struck up a long-lasting friendship.

Lexi squeezed the middle-aged man around his big aproned middle. "We're finally on a big case."

"Great. I hope we'll get to hear all about it at dinnertime," the gravelly-voiced New Yorker said. "Which reminds me, your parents are home. Dinner's in a few minutes. Go wash your hands, pronto." He accentuated the last word with a beat in the air from his large chopping knife.

The twins were proud of their famous parents, Dr. Ian Wyatt and Dr. Becky Marlton. They usually left for their jobs at the ARC at the same time every weekday and came home together, walking hand in hand or riding their bicycles. Lexi had her father's green eyes, dark hair, and love of ancient cultures. Lanny had inherited his mother's creative sensibilities, curly blonde hair, and unusual blue-violet eyes—"Liz Taylor eyes," as Uncle Rocky called them, referencing the beautiful, purple-eyed actress. Even though Elizabeth Taylor was a woman, Lanny couldn't be happier about the comparison. One of his hobbies was watching old Hollywood movies, and he admired all those stars from long ago. In fact, one of his all-time favorite actresses was Miss Taylor.

Soon, the five were seated around the enormous kitchen table that often accommodated neighbors or guests from the ARC. During the meal, Lexi and Lanny shared their first official case with the family. Their parents weren't ones to worry. Uncle Rocky worried plenty enough for everyone. Still, Dad didn't like the sound of a chase. "A theft is one thing," he said, "but I don't want you getting in over your heads."

"The police are handling that part, Dad," Lexi said. At Uncle Rocky's snorting sound, she continued, "Really. You can check with Moki's dad if you don't believe me." She had them there. She and her brother never lied. It was a point of pride for their parents.

"Okay, then," Dad said, "anything we can do to help?"

"Yes. Please explain to us what exactly happened to Dr. Thornsley," urged Lexi. She leaned over and tightly squeezed her father's lower arm with both hands. Hearing him wince in pain, she quickly released her grip. Grabbing flesh when exuberant was her bad habit.

"Well," he said as he set his fork down and massaged his arm. "It was last October when the theft occurred. Our family was out of town as you might remember. The urn Dr. Thornsley had found last summer in Egypt was on loan to the ARC from the British Museum in Cairo. It was stolen the very first night it arrived here."

"Some people still believe he stole it," said Mom with a pained look in her eyes.

"How could anyone believe that a man of Dr. Thornsley's character and reputation would do such a thing?" returned Uncle Rocky. He shook his big sphinxlike head.

Lanny asked, "Dad, do you and Mom believe Dr. Thornsley stole the urn?" He slathered more salsa across the enchilada on his plate.

"Not for a second. For one thing, all the evidence against him turned out to be circumstantial," replied Dad.

Lexi looked up from her meal. "Wait. What does 'circumstantial' mean?"

Lanny, the walking dictionary, pounced. "'Circum-stantial' means that the so-called evidence gathered was not determined to be worthy enough to be able to lead to an indisputable conviction of guilt in a court of law."

"Okay. Thanks, I think," Lexi said. Her brother was smarter than anyone else she knew, except for her parents, of course. But she didn't tell him too often, or it might go to his head.

Dad continued, "Besides, we will always feel, as does Uncle Rocky, that Dr. Thornsley was too honest and devoted to Egyptology and the laws and ethics of archaeology to ever commit such a crime."

"I still can't believe he's not with us anymore," Mom said with a catch in her voice.

"No one ever said how he died," Lanny nudged, hoping for information, not tears.

"Massive stroke," his dad explained. "Perhaps from being under a terrible strain for six months following the theft." He finished the last bite of tortilla left on his plate.

"What a waste of a terrific person and a great life," Uncle Rocky sighed, hauling his tall frame up from his chair to serve the ice cream dessert. The others passed their dinner plates to Dad who rose and set the stack by the sink.

"Get this," Lexi said. "While we were waiting for the police to arrive, Mrs. T shared some bad news she got this morning from Dr. Abbott. He told her Dr. T can't be honored at this summer's annual Paradise Days Festival. I just don't understand that." She scowled.

Dad returned to his seat. "Well, my princess, there are some people at the ARC and from the public in general who still have unfavorable opinions about Dr. Thornsley's part in the theft. They feel that until the urn is found and returned to the ARC, and until any possible culprit or culprits are arrested and convicted for its theft, doubts about Dr. Thornsley's innocence and integrity as a scientist will surely remain. Honoring a man who might be guilty could embarrass the ARC."

"That's so unfair," replied Lexi, pushing away her chocolate dessert with a pout.

"Who at the ARC is in charge of finalizing the festival honorees' list?" asked Lanny. He took a large bite of his ice cream.

Lexi had to admire her brother's many qualities. He could separate out his feelings and get down to the business at hand. That's what made him the leader of their detective agency.

"Dr. Abbott is the director, so he has the final say," replied Dad. "But he must take into consideration what the ARC's festival committee of scientists and art historians advises."

"Before you ask, your dad and I couldn't be on this year's nominating committee since we served last year," Mom said regretfully. Her ice cream was starting to resemble chocolate soup like Lexi's.

"Life just isn't fair sometimes, and that makes me angry," Lexi said, scowling more intensely now and slumping at her place.

"I know, sweetie," Mom replied. "But remember. You four kids are on the case now. That means you're doing your part to set matters right. Think positively." She stroked Lexi's hand.

"Which reminds me," said Lanny as he sat erectly. "We have our direction for tomorrow. The four Botanic Hill detectives' first stop will be the ARC to see Dr. Abbott."

# CHAPTER THREE

· ✧ ·

# Clues from the ARC

"**M**y dad says there are no leads yet on Mask Face and the blue getaway car, and all was quiet at Mrs. T's last night," Moki said. He had caught up with the other three kids in Dr. Abbott's roomy, high-ceilinged outer office. Giant fans twirled hypnotically above them causing heavenly breezes to cascade downward. They were early for their afternoon appointment at the ARC, and the director was elsewhere in a meeting.

"I'm glad for Mrs. T's sake that it was quiet," said Rani.

"Well, here's more about Mrs. T, but you won't be glad to hear it," Lexi said. She shifted to face her friends. "When I called her this morning to get permission to share her story with Dr. Abbott, she said she had more to tell us but had been interrupted yesterday by Mask Face and the police visit." Three pairs of wide eyes were now on her. "It seems that a couple of days ago, Mrs. T finally found the strength and the time to look at her old bank statements that were piled up from April and May. She noticed that the balance in one of her and Dr. T's savings accounts was much lower than she had remembered from when Dr. T was alive."

Lanny sprang to his feet, almost knocking over his chair. "How much lower?"

Lexi locked eyes with her brother. "50,000 dollars lower," she whispered.

"Yikes!" Rani said, causing Dr. Abbott's secretary, Paula Graham, to glance up from her work.

"Double yikes," Moki replied more softly as he sank onto a small sofa.

"Did she discuss that with the bank people?" Rani asked.

"Yeah. She said she called the bank, and an employee confirmed the new total. Not only that, but it seems Dr. T withdrew the money himself in five visits, 10,000 dollars each time, between the middle of February and the end of March."

Moki had been staring down at his flip-flops with a frown but quickly sat up. "Why would Dr. T do that and not tell Mrs. T? And in cash, not checks?"

"Yes, in cash. I also asked her your first question. She can't explain Dr. T's actions," Lexi replied. "What's more, she's searched the house but can't find the money. It's gone missing, too, just like the picture from Dr. T's study."

"Smells like extortion to me," Lanny said, still standing but now with his hands on his hips.

"That's exactly what I was thinking—that Dr. T was being blackmailed," Lexi replied. Her eyes couldn't decide between fire or tears.

Rani crossed her arms. "That stinks. Why would anyone do that to such a sweet man?"

"Extortion and blackmail do stink," replied Lanny. "And if this theory proves to be true, if that does in fact explain the money drain, then we're going to find out who did it and why."

At that moment, the director arrived wearing a suit and tie and carrying several folders under his left arm. He greeted his young friends, firmly pumping each one's hand. "Sorry to keep you waiting. Please, please come in." The polite Englishman pushed open his inner office door labeled, "Dr. Leland Abbott, Director, Antiquities Research Collective." They passed into his spacious, sun-saturated workplace that had the scent of a man's spicy cologne. "Paula, please hold any calls," he said over his shoulder to his secretary. He set his pile of work on his desktop.

"Will do, boss," Ms. Graham replied brightly before resuming her word processing.

Lexi returned the director's smile. She loved his British accent. "You didn't really keep us waiting, Dr. Abbott. We were early. Thanks for seeing us today. We didn't give you much notice."

"I'm honored. Please be seated," he said, motioning to

some chairs. Without asking, he poured each of them small cups of his favorite Darjeeling tea. The exotic, flowery aroma emanated from a sizable teapot brewing behind his immense desk. "What brings you four to the ARC today? A mystery finally afoot?" The director unbuttoned his suit jacket, sat down, savored a sip of his tea, and listened.

"That's right, Dr. A. Some serious business, I'm afraid," said Lanny. The boy began sharing all that Mrs. Thornsley had told them, including the mysterious incidents at her house and the missing money.

The twin finished by emphasizing that their assignment was to find and return the urn to the ARC, catch the real culprit or culprits, and have Dr. Thornsley's reputation restored. Lanny stressed that they hoped to do so in time for the Egyptologist to be honored at this year's summer festival.

"Well, Lanyon," Dr. Abbott replied, leaning forward with his hands clasped, "that's ambitious of all of you though I'm not surprised, given your logical tendencies and strong sense of responsibility. I applaud all of you for taking this case." Then his eyebrows furrowed. "It certainly seems that there have been some strange new developments in this mystery. For the record, I don't believe that Dr. Thornsley stole the urn. He was one of the finest men and most dedicated scientists I've ever known. His sudden death was tragic, indeed."

"It's good to know you feel that way," Lexi said. "But if so, why did you say Dr. T can't be honored at the festival?" There was an edge in her voice that she couldn't disguise.

"Ah, that's the problem with being in charge, Alexia. I can't always put my beliefs and feelings first. I must consider what others think. In this case, those on the ARC's festival committee and certain members of the larger scientific community. I do hope you understand."

"Well, yes, I guess. That's what my dad said you'd say," she replied in a hushed tone.

"Dr. Abbott, can you tell us more about Dr. Thornsley?" asked Rani. She leaned forward.

"Gladly, Rani. Dr. Thornsley was one of the few Egyptologists here who had specialized in Egypt's earliest eras, the Predynastic and Early Dynastic Periods from 5,000 years ago, and he was fascinated by one of Egypt's first pharaohs, Menes, and the cobra goddess Wadjet."

"Yes, he wrote a book about them, which is in his study," said Lexi sitting up in her chair. "He shared the pictures from it with me often. Can you tell us more about Menes and Wadjet?"

"Certainly. I know you want to become an Egyptologist yourself one day. Well, there exist many legends and exaggerated claims surrounding the pharaoh, Menes, who reigned for sixty-two years. He was credited with unifying Upper and Lower Egypt and with possibly inventing Egyptian writing. Supposedly, he died a horrible death when a Nile River hippo mauled him."

"Yuck," Lexi said, grimacing and unintentionally banging down her china teacup.

The director stifled a chuckle and continued. "Concerning Wadjet, she was the protector of Upper and Lower Egypt and of royalty. She was often represented as an Egyptian-cobra-headed woman called the *uraeus*, which rose protectively from the front of the headdresses and crowns of ancient rulers and deities to signify their sovereignty." As he spoke, the director stood to adjust the Venetian blinds against the strong sunlight that was now inundating his young guests.

"The missing urn is from Menes's time," he continued, "which is the main reason Dr. Thornsley was overseeing its visit here, and I should add what some consider to be a possible motive for Dr. Thornsley to steal it—that he simply wanted the priceless piece for himself."

Before his sister could utter a protest, Lanny said, "Dr. Abbott, we understand from Mrs. Thornsley that there was a mummy inside the urn. I believe it was a cobra?"

"That's correct, Lanyon. A mummified Egyptian cobra to be exact."

Moki fidgeted. "All this snake talk . . ." he mumbled.

"Snakes aren't your cup of tea, so to speak, Moki?" asked the director with a grin.

"That's an understatement, Dr. Abbott. Not in teacups, urns, or anywhere. I would like to know, though, if it was common for ancient Egyptians to bury mummified animals in tombs." Moki grabbed a tissue from the box on the director's desk to mop his now sweaty forehead.

"Yes, especially animals that represented deities such as Wadjet."

"Was anything else found in the urn?" Lanny asked.

"Scans showed bones and some rock-like objects, perhaps crystallized venom or linen wrappings from the decomposed snake. But it's hard to say without opening the urn."

"Mrs. Thornsley showed us a photo of the urn. How big was it?" asked Lexi.

"That was probably the photo that went viral," replied Dr. Abbott. "Nothing as exceptional as that urn has been discovered in quite some time. At any rate, the artifact is seven inches tall and five inches in diameter at its middle. You probably noticed that it has golden painted lotus swirls, the cartouche of Menes, as well as the hieroglyphics of Wadjet on the front of the black urn." He started to reach for a book of hieroglyphics to show the detectives, but Rani had a question.

"What's a cartouche?"

Lanny jumped at his chance. "A cartouche is an oblong shape that encloses hieroglyphics." Dr. Abbott nodded, but the kids rolled their eyes. "Lanny the Lexicon" was at it again.

Then they gathered around the director who had opened the book. Sunlight glinted off the colorful pages.

"I can't wait to see those hieroglyphics on the actual urn," said Rani. She smiled and caressed the image of Wadjet on the page with her finger. Moki's hands, however, were clasped behind his back.

"And I have every reason to believe that you will," replied Dr. Abbott, "given the Botanic Hill Detectives' sterling reputation for apprehending thieves as you did in Paris." He replaced the book on a nearby shelf. "I regret not having asked you myself to tackle the case earlier."

"That's all right, Dr. Abbott. At least we're on the job now," said Lanny with a smile.

"Can you tell us about the theft of the urn?" Rani asked.

"Yes. Dr. Thornsley had locked the urn in his office cabinet. The next morning, none of us had any luck opening the padlock. In fact, Dr. Thornsley noticed that it wasn't the same padlock he used the night before, so we cut it off. When the cabinet was finally opened, the urn had vanished."

Lanny heard Lexi sigh heavily and was concerned all of this talk about Dr. Thornsley had overwhelmed her. She and the Egyptologist had been such good friends. Time to end the meeting. He said, "You've shared some fascinating and valuable information with us today, Dr. Abbott. We appreciate your support and won't take up any more of your time this afternoon." The boy stood, and the others, including the director, followed his lead.

"I'll make you four an offer," said Dr. Abbott. "It's now late June. If you can find the stolen urn and prove Dr. Thornsley's innocence by the end of July, I'll do all I can to ensure that his reputation is restored in time for him to be recognized at the festival this summer." The director smiled broadly and returned his teacup to its saucer with a clink.

"That's fabulous news. You can count on us," replied a beaming Lexi.

"Now, let me walk all of you out. I must find Dr.

Granger to see what progress he's made on our festival exhibit."

Moki carefully passed the stack of teacups and saucers he had collected to Dr. Abbott. Lexi was a bit nervous since Moki wasn't always the most graceful person around finery. She often teased him about this, saying he was like a swaying Hawaiian palm tree in a china shop. Fortunately, there were no mishaps this time.

The four followed the chief director down the hall, passing the twins' parents' offices. There were their doors' golden nameplates: "Dr. Ian Wyatt, Director of Archaeology" and "Dr. Rebecca Marlton, Director of Art History." Dr. Abbott smiled as Lexi first gave her father's nameplate and then her mother's a quick polishing with her sweatshirt sleeve. "Your parents aren't in their offices right now," he said. "As always, they're hard at work elsewhere in the building."

Next, they passed Dr. Thornsley's old office. Lexi shivered. His tarnished nameplate that seemed forever bonded to that door had somehow been removed. In its place was a shiny new one that read, "Dr. Bret Granger, Director of Egyptology." She jerked away, deciding not to give as much as another glance at the office of the young Egyptologist, who she felt had too hurriedly taken Dr. Thornsley's place. She corrected herself. No. No one could ever really take his place.

When they descended to the marble-tiled first floor lobby, Lanny immediately spied Dr. Granger standing next to someone. He didn't like the grumpy scientist any more than Lexi did. The tall man was always snapping at people and acting self-important. Lanny had never heard him say one kind word to or about Dr. Thornsley.

Lanny asked the director, "Who's that woman with Dr. Granger?"

"That's Ms. Augusta Ramsey, the owner of Ancient Sands Curio Shop," replied Dr. Abbott. "Dr. Granger has asked her to help him plan and set up the ARC's festival exhibit. She has many Egyptian-themed props in her old shop on Jacaranda Street to help make a more authentic-looking display."

Uncharacteristically, Lanny let his feelings get the better of him. He instantly distrusted Augusta Ramsey. Her slender face, long beak-like nose, dark, lustrous hair, and black clothes made Lanny picture a raven. Adding to his suspicion was his observation that as she and Dr. Granger whispered off in a corner, she appeared to fidget and glance around nervously instead of giving the scientist her full attention.

"Well, I'll leave you young people to your task," said Dr. Abbott as he shook their hands. "Farewell for now and good luck. Thank you for filling me in on your big case. Please let me know if I can be of further assistance. And I hope that you'll keep me informed of your progress," added the director. They assured him that they would. He then walked quickly toward the pair conferring in the corner.

# CHAPTER FOUR

· ◇ ·

# Snakes and Shakes

Rani and Lexi stayed behind at the ARC to observe Ms. Ramsey and Dr. Granger while Moki and Lanny headed for the zoo on a fact-finding mission about snakes. Lanny never missed an opportunity to push Moki out of his comfort zone, and this trip should do the trick. At that moment, the boys sat with Dr. Tessa Kurtz, curator of herpetology. Dr. Kurtz's legs dangled over the edge of the long polished-metal table in the center of the room where she sat with her two guests surrounded by more than thirty snakes, all behind glass. Her khaki pants, polo shirt with the zoo's emblem on the pocket, and laced-up hiking boots made the redheaded scientist look as if she had just returned from an African safari. Most of the snakes around them were highly venomous. Lanny seemed almost as calm as the herpetologist. Moki was another story. He was sorry he had let Lanny talk him into coming. Try as he might, he was not able to will away the beads of perspiration that were erupting from his forehead.

Frequent rustling sounds reminded Moki where he was, and it was no longer the ARC. As if he needed reminding. "Tell me again why we're here in this snake house." He shifted positions to keep an eye on the where-abouts of the reptiles. "Couldn't we have just called or texted Dr. Kurtz instead? Isn't that one of the joys of technology?"

"No, bro. Nothing like the real thing—snakes or people. Dr. Abbott was talking about Egyptian cobras today, remember? So, I wanted to ask Dr. Kurtz about them in person. She's an authority on cobras and snake venom, and we're lucky enough to have her right here at our zoo."

"Thanks for the compliment, Lanny," the perky her-petologist replied. "This isn't exactly a snake house, Moki. It's the zoo's Reptile Care Facility. All these snakes you see here in their terraria are under special observation for medical or environmental purposes."

Lanny added, "You see, Dr. Kurtz, Moki's from Hawai'i and, as you know, there aren't any snakes there."

"Well then, Moki, it's probably natural that you would be afraid of reptiles at first. I know it might be useless to tell you to relax, but try, if possible. You're perfectly safe in here."

"Afraid *at first*? That's the second understatement regarding snakes I've heard today," Moki said. "Sounds like too much *pilikia* for me. Uh, that's Hawaiian for 'trouble.' All this hissing and slithering I'm hearing—what happened to *Snakes 101*, the gentle introductory course? This is more like *Snakes 501*—hands-on with prior knowledge required." His face contorted as if he'd eaten something highly disgusting.

"Face your fears, Moki. Get out of your comfort zone," the scientist replied with her legs still swinging casually.

"Easy for you to say—with all due respect, Dr. Kurtz. You aren't afraid of snakes."

"Not true, Moki. I am afraid of them. Actually, it's more respect than fear. That's what keeps me safe. I know their dangers. But to me, they have a beauty unlike any other animal. Now, let's get back to why you're here. Unfortunately, I can't spare much time for you two today. This morning's earthquake has kept me very busy checking the Reptile House enclosures for cracks. Don't want to take any chances with these aging buildings. And you've got that we're-on-our-first-case look," she said, scooting off the tabletop. The boys followed.

"We are. We'd like to know about Egyptian cobras," Lanny said while glancing around.

"You've come to the right place. We have a visiting Egyptian cobra right in here. She's our guest from the Cactusville Reptile Gardens." Dr. Kurtz pointed across the room to a terrarium against the opposite wall. Moki was content to stay right where he was as long as possible.

"From Cactusville? But that's out in the desert, sixty miles east of here," said Lanny.

"There have been some problems out there. I don't

have all the details, but we're giving some of their cobras a home temporarily. The scientists also sent us some vials of venom, which we don't normally store here. Venom is used to make antivenin and other medicines, but that's not what we do here at the zoo. You see, we study and display our snakes for educational purposes. We don't milk them."

"Whoa. Okay—wait. Milk a snake? What's that all about?" asked Moki. Lanny grinned, thinking that if Moki's eyebrows got any higher, they'd reach his hairline.

"Moki, 'milking' a snake means to take its venom," Lanny replied. "They make the snake bite down over a cup, which causes it to extrude . . . that means give up its venom. Then they use it to make antivenin, or as some call it, anti-venom." Lanny tried to demonstrate the procedure with his fingers squeezing down on an imaginary snake's head over a nearby laboratory beaker.

"Uh, that's not a job I'll ever be doing," Moki replied, pulling back from his friend. "And by the way, bro, no more new words today, please. I'm still trying to digest '*milk* a snake.'"

Lanny was unfazed by Moki and was fearless of reptiles. He walked right over to the Egyptian cobra's large terrarium and put his nose against the glass. The snake stared at him for a while, then reared up and displayed her hood in warning. Moki tried to pull him back. "Dude, stop. You're making it mad."

"There's glass there, bro. It won't get us." Lanny grinned and slapped Moki on the back.

"Careful. That's Wadjet you're getting riled up there, guys. Queen Cleopatra didn't get off easily when she stuck her hand into a basket of figs that contained an Egyptian cobra. But she was killing herself intentionally to avoid capture by the Roman army." The boys' hiked-up eyebrows caught the herpetologist's attention. "Yes, from a cobra's bite, not an asp's. History didn't get that right."

"Wadjet—named after the Egyptian cobra goddess?" Moki asked from a few yards away.

"That's right. Isn't she a beauty?" Dr. Kurtz asked, staring at Wadjet, who was again slithering. "Just look at her gray-brown coloring and markings, black eyes, and perfect scales."

Lanny got right to the point of their visit. "Dr. Kurtz, a question. Is it possible for 5,000-year-old Egyptian cobra venom from a mummified snake to still be potent?"

"Wow, I don't get asked that every day." She cradled her chin between her thumb and index finger. "Oh," she said, straightening up. "This must be related to that mummified cobra that went missing from the ARC last fall. Well, to be honest, I would seriously question its potency after five millennia. Studies have shown, however, that snake venom can still be potent after one hundred years. But . . . maybe if that ancient snake and its venom had been preserved just right, and if any collected venom was later rehydrated in a certain way and injected, it might cause some damage. What a fascinating study. I'd do just about anything to get my hands on that snake to find out!"

"How deadly is cobra venom?" Lanny pressed.

In answer, Dr. Kurtz put on surgical gloves and took out a vial from the Cactusville batch in the refrigerator. Moki joined them more out of wanting safety in numbers than from any sense of curiosity.

"Egyptian cobra venom is very lethal, more powerful than a king cobra's, but a bite from either snake can kill," Dr. Kurtz said as she gently swirled the vial of golden liquid. "It only takes a drop of this stuff to do the trick. Venom usually has to be injected to be harmful, but it can also be absorbed into the blood stream through an internal or external wound and cause death."

"Oh, great. Li'l ol' me in here in the same room with snakes that can kill elephants," said Moki as he inched his way closer to the door.

"You aren't exactly 'little,' bro," Lanny replied with a grin. "You eat too many cookies."

"True on both counts but not very comforting," his friend returned, still eyeing the door.

"Moki, as long as there's glass between you and the snakes, you're perfectly safe," said Dr. Kurtz. She returned the vial to its refrigerated rack. Moki stared at her, expressionless.

"Dr. Kurtz, if that vial of Egyptian cobra venom hadn't been labeled, would you still be able to tell what kind of a snake it came from?" asked Lanny.

"Absolutely. It's done using what we herpetologists call phylogenetic analysis, or analyzing the components of the venom. Different snake species have different components."

"Somehow your vocabulary lessons are easier to take than Lanny's," Moki added.

Just then, the wall phone rang by the door where Moki was standing. Lanny and the herpetologist moved toward it. Dr. Kurtz picked up the phone and listened with wrinkled brows. After giving the caller some directions, she hung up.

Almost instantly following the call, the building started to shake mildly. The three of them instinctively grabbed hold of the nearby metal table for support.

"Here we go again. An aftershock! I've been afraid this would happen," said Dr. Kurtz. She rapidly surveyed the room full of terraria. "And one of my assistants just called to say he's found a somewhat hidden but large crack from this morning's tremor on one of our venomous snake enclosure's glass panes. It's a major emergency. Come out with me quickly boys—now! I have to attend to this immediately," she shouted behind her, as she grabbed her tool bag, yanked open the heavy door, and fled outside and down the breezeway to the enclosure.

Unfortunately, Moki and Lanny weren't as fast as Dr. Kurtz. The door banged shut in their surprised faces and locked. They were trapped in a windowless room.

As if that weren't bad enough, the power failed simultaneously, and the room went pitch black. Both boys froze, helplessly surrounded by three walls of venomous snakes they could still hear but no longer see.

# CHAPTER FIVE

· ✧ ·

# Hissing in the Dark

Meanwhile, the two girls arrived back at Quince Street having little information to report from their observations at the ARC.

"Hi, Uncle Rocky," Lexi said. The man was busy folding laundry while sitting at one of the backyard patio tables. She bent down to his level and draped an arm around his shoulders.

"Hello, girls. What a hot afternoon. Did you feel the little aftershock a while ago?" Before they could answer, he followed up with, "Hey, where are the boys?"

"You mean they aren't back yet?" Lexi asked. "They left us at three-thirty to go see the curator of reptiles at the zoo." She glanced down at her mobile phone to check for any calls.

"Well, it's only four-thirty," the man said. "The boys know to be back by five. They'll probably come strolling in anytime now. Dinner's at six as usual," he said. He folded another pair of socks into a ball, which he flung into the basket.

"Mmm, I smell garlic. What's for dinner tonight? Italian?" Lexi asked, licking her lips.

"Spaghetti à la Rocky, power greens with balsamic vinaigrette dressing, oven-broiled garlic bread, and ice cream sundaes with fresh fruit for dessert," replied the cook. "And don't bother asking me what the *à la Rocky* part means. It's due to the secret ingredient that shall remain a secret," he returned. But his bark quickly turned into a smile. He never could seem to get even a little firm with Lexi, who had him wrapped around her finger ever since she was a baby.

"Sounds yummy to me, secret or no secret," said Rani, picking up a clean sock ball and lobbing it to her friend.

"Thanks. I think so, too," he replied with his typically sly smile.

"Hey, Uncle Rocky. Did you know that Rani is a synesthete?" Lexi asked, watching for the man's reaction. She always looked forward to showing off her knowledge for him.

He paused and looked at Rani with surprise. "So, you have synesthesia? I've never met anyone who does—until now, that is. This is great. I wish I had it. What type do you have?"

"I taste food when I hear a name or word. Like when I hear the name 'Uncle Rocky,' I taste those super-sweet Easter eggs that have that sugary marshmallow filling and that crusty candy shell. In your case, the shell is turquoise."

Sherrill Joseph

"Well, you've just confirmed what I keep telling everyone around here—that I'm extra, extra sweet," the man replied with a grin.

"And a good egg, ha ha," Lexi added, smiling. "But never crusty. So, how can we help with dinner?" She leaned in and spread all her fingertips on the patio tabletop. Ever since all four kids were little, their parents expected them to do chores. By now, it was a well-ingrained habit.

"You can start by not getting that pair of socks dirty that you're throwing. Then you can set the dining room table. Let's see. There'll be us five, and the Kumars—that's three more—and the Kalanis—that's two more. Your tutor, Bruce, is still out of town. So just ten tonight." The Wyatts hosted a dining room full of dinner guests at least once a week, and tonight was company night with their special neighbors.

"Will do. Candles, too," replied both girls. Rani tossed the sock ball back into the laundry basket. "We'll even put the folded clothes away for you upstairs, Uncle Rocky," she said.

"Be my guests," he replied, accentuating the last word and sweeping his hand grandly over the hefty pile.

"BFF, have you ever noticed that it's more fun to do chores when it's your idea, not someone else's?" Lexi asked.

"All the time," Rani replied, scrunching up her lips and reaching for the basket.

"Then I encourage you two girls to keep having those ideas," said the beaming cook.

The girls each grabbed a side of the basket, bounded indoors, and dashed up the back staircase where their raucous laughter outdid their pounding footsteps.

"This isn't *Snakes 501*—it's *Snakes 911* . . . for emergency," said Moki through rivers of perspiration. They were still without power and in the dark inside the Reptile Care Facility. "I didn't sign on for this. To quote myself, 'Sounds like much *pilikia* to me.' I've never been so sorry about being so right."

The two boys had wisely decided to stay where they were by the sealed door. They worried that any movement on their part might upset one or more of the snake enclosures. They had slid straight down onto the floor with their backs against the heavy exit door, tired from unsuccessfully shouting and banging to get someone's attention. They'd had no luck calling from their mobile devices. Lanny carefully reached for the wall phone above them one more time.

"Aww, this phone's still dead, too," Lanny said, slowly reaching to replace it on its hook.

"Hey, don't use the word 'dead' in here, bro," whispered Moki, grabbing Lanny's arm. "If you must use that word, say *all pau* instead. Means the same thing, and the snakes probably don't know Hawaiian."

"And maybe the power failure is more widespread than we know. I guess everyone's too busy dealing with the enclosure problem. But don't worry, Moki. Someone will come for us soon." When it came to bluffing, Lanny had as much skill as Uncle Rocky, which was nil.

"Yeah, right. You're looking at one hopeful Hawaiian. Make that you're *listening* to one hopeful Hawaiian. I don't want my dad to lose me, his only son. I'm all he's got left now that my mom's gone. Plus, I don't want to lose me, either."

Moki had lost his mother in a car accident. That was the main reason his dad moved him to California. His dad said it was too hard, living in the same house and driving all the same streets in Honolulu without her. Lanny felt his own heart break every time Moki brought up his mom. He wouldn't have known his best friend if they hadn't moved to California, but the reason for the move . . . It was all too sad.

Moki quickly changed the subject. "Hey, the girls know where we are! If we aren't home on time, Lexi will put it together and bring help." He managed a toothy grin, invisible in their present situation.

"Speaking of Lexi, have I detected a slight crush on your part for my one and only dear little sister, bruh?" Lanny asked. He was trying to change the subject, mainly for Moki's sake.

"Yeah, bruh. Kind of like the one you have on Rani," Moki returned, grinning more.

"You know, one of these days, instead of calling you *bro*, maybe I'll be calling you *bro-in-law*." Lanny nudged his friend as much as he dared, egging on a mock fight in perhaps the only venue where he could get away with it. He knew full well that muscular Moki wouldn't risk a scuffle under the current circumstances.

"Very funny. If we don't get out of here soon, Lexi will be my widow before she's my bride. I'd ask you to take it outside so we could settle this man to man, but the door's locked."

After a moment of silence that seemed to stretch on forever, Lanny asked, "So what do you think Rani tastes when she hears the word 'snakes'?"

"I don't know about her, but I taste Death with a capital D. . . . I mean, *all pau*," Moki replied. "Hey, wait—did you hear that?" The playful tone was gone from his voice.

"You mean that hissing and movement coming from the snakes?"

"Exactly. They're wide awake and probably hearing what we're saying. They know where we are. Let's stop talking." Moki gripped Lanny's arm hard.

"Moki, snakes can't hear. They sense location with their tongues using their prey's body heat and motions to track them down. And by the way, where did you learn that annoying arm-gripping technique—from Lexi?" Lanny attempted to peel Moki's strong hands off himself.

Moki passed over Lanny's last question but released his grip. "Okay, we've got the motion part squared away since we're not moving. Let's focus on the body heat angle next. We've always told everyone we're two cool dudes. Now, we need to be 'too cool' in the other way—as in very frozen solid."

"You're *pupule*," Lanny said, using Moki's Hawaiian word for "crazy."

"I'd rather be *pupule* and alive than sane and dead. Oops, I just used the D word again."

The two sat in dark silence for a few more minutes. Then Moki asked slowly, "Do you think Dr. Kurtz might have left us in here on purpose?"

"Huh? Whatever could make you think that crazy idea, bro?"

"Because of something she said right before she left us in here to die—that she'd 'do just about anything to get her hands on that mummified snake.'"

# CHAPTER SIX

· ✧ ·

# Dinnertime Excursion

Uncle Rocky met Lexi and Rani in the kitchen as he walked back toward the stove from the dining room. "Great job setting the table, girls. Hey, and I like your tattoos, Lexi." Rani had painted henna tattoos on Lexi's arms after they finished their chores. Uncle Rocky gave them two thumbs up. "Now, if those pets would just get down here for their dinner, I'd be even happier. Pharaoh, Cleo, soup's on!" he shouted up the back staircase. This was a nightly ritual.

"No one ever seems to call Pharaoh by his real name anymore," Lexi said to Rani. "King Ramesses II, that's what my dad named him." Her eyes were glued on the backstairs, not on Rani.

"How come they don't?" Rani asked, joining Lexi in gazing at the same spot. "His real name is so cool."

"Yeah, my dad thought it was only right to name our dog after one of Egypt's greatest pharaohs, being an archaeologist. But the nickname stuck as soon as we got him home from the rescue shelter. Now watch. He never misses a meal. I guess border collies have big appetites."

As if on cue, Pharaoh came bounding down the stairs, tripping over himself. Then he looked up, panting expectantly while whining at Uncle Rocky, and running circles around his legs. As usual, however, their Abyssinian cat was still nowhere to be seen.

"Well, the chow hound is here, and I know how to get that finicky feline to come prancing," the cook said as he opened a can of smelly tuna. The whir of the electric can opener did the trick. Cleo made her composed entrance, as if imitating her royal namesake, Queen Cleopatra VII.

"Your royal majesties," said Uncle Rocky, appearing to bow as he set their food dishes down side by side on the floor. Pharaoh chomped with unrestrained gusto. Cleo nibbled with superb indifference.

"Girls, I'm worried about the boys," said Uncle Rocky, glancing up at the wall clock. "It's five-thirty. They should have been home a half-hour ago. It's not like them to be late and not call."

Just then the twins' parents entered the kitchen to assist with dinner. "Lexi, did your brother tell you where they were going? I thought you four were spending the day together," asked Becky Marlton, her arms crossed.

"We were all together until about three-thirty when we split up, Mom. Lanny and Moki said they were going to the zoo to talk with the curator of reptiles, except Lanny used a different word, as usual—*herpet* something. Rani and I stayed longer at the ARC." She pulled on her mother's arms.

"Did the boys indicate to either of you that they knew what time to be home?" asked Ian Wyatt standing next to the twins' mom. His six-foot, three-inch height made him tower over his wife.

"Oh, yes, Dr. W," replied Rani. "They definitely said they'd be here by five. And I've already tried calling and texting both of them a bunch of times. No answers yet."

At that moment the front doorbell rang. "That must be our boys home safe and sound now," Rocky said, dropping his stirring spoon and moving faster than normal out of the kitchen.

"It's more likely our dinner guests have arrived. I doubt the boys would ring the doorbell, anyway," called Dr. Marlton.

Friendly voices were heard in the living room, and the cook, who was trying to appear cheerful, arrived back in the fragrant kitchen with Dr. and Mrs. Kumar and Sergeant Kalani in tow.

"Hi, Gajara, Devi, Dan," Becky Marlton said. "Welcome. Come in and relax."

"It's good to be here," Rani's mother, Gajara Kumar, sighed. She was a taller version of her equally kind, beautiful daughter.

The guests were instantly tempted by the soft chairs around the cooking island and the large platter of veggie hors d'oeuvres. But greeting their children first was more important.

Rani and Lexi rushed toward Gajara Kumar and hugged her tightly.

Mrs. Kumar stroked each girl's hair. "Thanks. I needed that. Big day at the airport."

Lexi looked up at her and responded, "Good, Mrs. K. I hope that means during dinner, you'll tell us more stories about being an airline manager. It always sounds so, well . . . glamorous."

"Not always as glamorous as you think," she replied with a chuckle, squeezing them closer.

"Hey! Where are my hugs?" Devi Kumar asked. "I had to hang out at the university all day."

The girls ran to embrace him. "We figured as much, Dad, you being a geologist and the earthquake and all," Rani said with a grin. "Poor old Dad, having to work on a Saturday."

Moki's dad, Sergeant Kalani, or Sergeant Dan as he was known in the community, didn't wait for his hugs or any sympathy. His alert police-officer eyes had noticed something unusual.

"Hey, where are the boys?" he asked.

Lexi's dad told all the parents the boys had not come home yet. The adults decided to call the zoo, which Dr. Wyatt did immediately. Returning to the kitchen, he said, "Well, that was useless. I got the taped message that said the zoo was closed and to call back tomorrow."

Sergeant Dan was concerned. "My squad car is right outside. Let's head to the zoo and see if we can contact anyone there on the way."

The two girls started to follow the sergeant out, but the adults thought it best that everyone stay at the house except Moki's dad and the twins' parents. The girls were disappointed but obeyed.

"Besides, you two girls can entertain Rani's parents until we get back," Becky Marlton said. "Rani, how about showing them the gorgeous henna tattoos that you made on Lexi? Rocky, please keep everything warm as best you can, okay?"

"Not to worry, Dr. M," he said. "Will do. Just bring our boys home safe and sound."

"Mom, I'm really worried about Lanny and Moki," cried Lexi, pulling on her mother's arm again, her eyes tearing up.

"Don't worry, pumpkin. I'm sure they're fine. We'll find them," she replied with her artist's fingertips caressing her daughter's face. Then the three adults headed to the car.

Once the twins' parents were settled in the back seat, Sergeant Dan quickly located the zoo's emergency number and called it. He got through to a night watchman. "This is Sergeant Daniel Kalani with the Las Palmitas Police Department. We're looking for two boys, aged thirteen, answering to the first names of Lanny and Moki, who might still be in the zoo, probably with the curator of herpetology. Would you check on that immediately for me, please?"

"I think everyone's gone home, sergeant, but I'll certainly try," was the reply.

"We're on the way and will meet you by the zoo's entrance in a few minutes."

By the time the three arrived at the zoo, Mr. Willis, the elderly watchman, was waiting for them. "Sorry, but no one answered at the Reptile House. I'm not surprised because most of the zoo's power has been out. It's been a rough day here what with the heat, earthquake, and aftershock." The man shook his head.

"We'll need to search the area then and see if we can find the boys or the curator," said Sergeant Dan as he slammed the patrol car door shut and let out Becky and Ian.

Mr. Willis led the three parents to the Reptile House where they found Dr. Kurtz and a number of her assistants working feverishly to repair a snake enclosure. Its reptile occupants now squirmed safely in a burlap sack nearby. Emergency floodlights were ready. "Dr. Kurtz, these folks think their two boys might still be here with you," he said, pointing a thumb toward the parents.

Dr. Kurtz looked up for a split second, then resumed her work. "What boys?" she asked. The curator's entire attention had been focused on the repair job for over an hour now.

But then, it hit her. The blood immediately drained from her face. "Oh, my gosh!" she said, dropping a large roll of duct tape that had encircled her arm. "Do you mean Lanny and Moki?"

"Yes. Do you know where they are?" asked the sergeant as calmly as possible.

"I'm not positive, but I have a pretty good idea. Let's hurry. Follow me." Tessa Kurtz led the group at a run to the Reptile Care Facility and called outside the door, "Moki, Lanny, are you in there?"

"Aww! Yes! Thank goodness you're back. It's kind of weird in here," Lanny's voice, usually full of confidence, quavered.

Dr. Kurtz was unable to open the door using the electronic passcode system, but her good old-fashioned keys did the job. The boys tumbled out of the darkness, happy to be free.

"Oh, you guys, I'm so sorry. Are you all right? I thought you came out with me when I ran to deal with the emergency. You must be scared to death." Dr. Kurtz nervously glanced into the darkness behind them.

"No big deal," returned Moki, now standing tall. "Just *Snakes 911*."

Dr. Marlton took both of the boys in her arms and hugged them. "Oh, my two sweet *keiki*," she said, using the Hawaiian word for "children." "Are you sure you're all right?"

"I don't know about Lanny, but I could use another hug or two, California Mom," Moki replied to Becky Marlton, who gladly obliged him. He loved the attention she always showered upon him, but he especially enjoyed feeling as if he still had a mom, thanks to her. He called the Wyatts "fam" or the Hawaiian equivalent, *ohana*.

Next, Sergeant Dan got between the boys, locked one of his arms around each boy's neck, and cuffed them on their chins. When he was finished, Dr. Wyatt slapped each of them on the back, pulled them toward himself, and tousled their hair.

"Enough already, you guys," Lanny said, feigning anger and smoothing his curls.

"Personally, I like the attention," Moki replied with no exaggeration.

Dr. Kurtz apologized profusely to everyone and explained what had happened. "The glass had actually cracked in the highly venomous black mambas' enclosure. My attention there was essential and urgent. Guess I had a one-track mind."

Everyone understood and was just glad all turned out all right. The boys thanked Dr. Kurtz for the information she had given them earlier about venom and cobras. But they made no secret of the fact that they were glad to be able to put some distance now between the zoo and themselves.

"You boys really kept your heads in there. Not moving around was a brilliant strategy," said Dr. Kurtz with a hand on each boy's shoulder.

"Thanks. That's because we wanted to keep our lives," Moki replied, glancing up at the great outdoors, appreciating the few stars that were preparing for their nightly twinklefest.

The curator slowly flashed some light around inside the care facility to check for any issues.

The beam fell squarely upon the Egyptian cobra's cage.

The boys glanced in that direction and saw Wadjet raised up, hood extended, with her beady black eyes leering at them.

"Is she warning us or protecting us?" Moki asked. "Since I'm not an ancient Egyptian pharaoh, I'll assume she's warning us and take the hint. Thanks, Wadjet. I love you, too."

Turning to Lanny he said, "I'm just glad I didn't picture that happening while we were trapped in there, bruh."

"You and me both, bruh! You and me both," his friend replied.

# CHAPTER SEVEN

· ✧ ·

# Light Show

The four kids were now safely seated in the Botanic Hill Detectives Agency office following the zoo mishap. Their headquarters at Lanny and Lexi's was a slightly dusty garret at the top of a steep flight of stairs, accessed through a narrow door on the third floor. Its tiny attic window was the perfect place to observe anyone crossing over the Quince Street Footbridge, which spanned flower-strewn Lotus Canyon from the western border of Cortez Park. The public bridge was accessible from just beyond the north-eastern corner of the Wyatt-Marlton property.

From their usual places on the threadbare Persian rug, the four settled in with the soft, somehow reassuring, amber glow from an old lamp. Pharaoh and Cleo were reclining on their floor pillows. Rani and Lexi had run to Rani's house right after Uncle Rocky's fabulous Italian dinner to get her pet desert tortoise, Tortuga. It now rested comfortably on Moki's lap. This was her preferred spot. He had just finished writing their case goals on the whiteboard, which was propped on its tripod stand: "Find urn. Return it. Get thieves. Clear Dr. T."

Lanny had begun the meeting as head detective, a position earned from nonstop intelligent, logical thinking. "Okay, group, let's run it down. What do we have so far?" he had asked.

The group had a lot to discuss after the day's clue-gathering and from what Moki kept calling his "escape from the fangs of death" a little over an hour ago. They summarized their operating theories from the events that had occurred at Mrs. Thornsley's, the ARC, and the zoo. Then they developed a list of possible suspects and their motives and began planning their next steps. As agency secretary, Moki took notes on his tablet, so he could send them to the three friends afterwards.

"The missing money has me very concerned," Lanny said, tracing a finger over one of the faded patterns on the rug. "Somehow, I think the other events are tied into it. Again, it's just a feeling for now. We'll need proof, but experience tells me that's the angle for us to follow."

Lexi said, "Well, the one thing we do know for sure is Dr. T didn't steal the urn. That's a fact. No additional proof needed." She glanced hard at her evidence-driven brother.

"Won't argue with you on that, sis. Dr. T was too honest and ethical to steal any artifact, especially Egyptian. Say, did you girls learn anything new after Moki and I left you at the ARC?"

Rani answered with a frown, "I heard Dr. Granger say that he, 'a younger man,' was finally in charge of the Egyptology department now that 'the old man' was gone. Ms. Ramsey smiled."

"I realize he and Ms. Ramsey are supposed to be working together on the ARC's festival exhibit, but I don't trust Dr. Granger. It's just a feeling," Lexi added quickly, anticipating her brother's chronic requests for evidence. Her head told her that Lanny was correct. Good detective work required proof. For that reason, she knew Lanny would always be a better detective than she could ever hope to be. Lexi brought too much heart to her work. She wrestled with her belief that her brother brought too much brain. Actually, their first case was always showing the twins that balance would be key. Acting upon that compromise, however, would be another matter.

"Both Dr. Granger and Ms. Ramsey might require further investigation, anyway. We'll have to do so carefully so as not to inadvertently transmit our intentions . . . that means not to accidentally share our plans," Lanny said.

"'Inadvertently?' Really, bro? Once and for all, no more new words. My brain and my stomach are both full." Moki's head and shoulders slumped. Pharaoh let out an affirming bark, and the squad laughed it off.

But Lexi couldn't help a dig. "Wait. Moki, did I hear you right? Did you just say your stomach was full? That's a first." The two exchanged tight-lipped smiles and narrowed eyes.

"So, where do we go from here?" Rani asked. She glanced over to check on Tortuga.

"Let's head east to the Cactusville Reptile Gardens since Dr. Kurtz had mentioned there were some problems out there," replied Lanny. "Who knows? It could provide us with a lead. Besides, Moki and I haven't had enough reptiles yet," he said, punching Moki's arm.

Moki let out a big groan and would have fallen over sideways for dramatic effect had Tortuga not been nestled so comfortably on his lap. "More *pilikia*! What comes after *Snakes 911*? On second thought, don't answer that."

"So, Moki, how is it you're so afraid of snakes but not of Tortuga?" Rani asked.

"Simple. Tortuga's not a snake. She doesn't slither or have fangs of death. Besides, she reminds me of the *honu*—'sea turtles'—from back home on Oʻahu," the boy replied. He stroked Tortuga's bumpy shell. "I used to swim with them. They're respected by the Hawaiian people."

"Hey, bro, no more new words today, remember?" Lanny jabbed.

"But she's still a reptile," Rani pressed. She and Lexi watched for the boy's reaction.

"Uh, I try not to think about that family connection," Moki said. "Ignorance can be bliss."

"I think I'm going to start calling you 'Tortoise Man,'" Lanny teased, grinning at his friend.

"Say, I like it, but in sounds better in Hawaiian. Prepare for a word lesson, bro. *Honu-Kāne*. That's how we would say it in the Aloha state. Yeah. *Honu-Kāne*. That works for me," Moki replied, sitting up very tall and giving Lanny an equally smug grin back.

At that moment, there was a knock at the office door. Uncle Rocky squeezed in, carrying a tray of brownies and four glasses of milk. "Here, I thought you kids could use these after the big day all of you had. And, anyway, I want to hear more about how you're gonna solve your case."

"It's always the right time for second desserts," Moki replied, eyeing the cook's treat.

"I suspected you four could choke down some chocolate," the cook said, lowering the tray.

"I suspect you're right," Lexi replied. She reached for the biggest treat before Moki could.

Uncle Rocky did his best to join the kids on the floor but resorted to an old, overstuffed club chair instead. No sooner had the man gotten settled when Rani's expression changed.

"What's that?" she said.

Flashing lights were beaming into the attic through the little window and dancing wildly around the room. The squad quickly clustered around the opening.

Lanny grabbed the binoculars hanging nearby and trained them on the source. It took some time before the light show stopped interfering with his vision. "It's Mask Face! On the Quince Street Footbridge!" he shouted, lowering the binoculars.

Lexi yanked them from her brother, taking his neck

along with the strap, and aimed them out the window. "You're right. Eww! It's creepy," she replied as goosebumps ran down her arms.

The figure had turned the flashlight onto its mask, creating the illusion of a disembodied head floating across the bridge.

"What do you see? What do you see?" asked Uncle Rocky, craning his neck in their direction. Moki had plopped Tortuga into Uncle Rocky's lap before racing to the window. The man's twisting almost dumped the tortoise into the leftover brownies.

"It wants our attention, so let's give it to him—or her," said Moki, and the four were off, not having satisfied the cook's curiosity. They clambered down three flights of stairs with the dog at their heels, barking wildly. They ran past their startled parents in the living room and toward the front door. Meanwhile, Uncle Rocky was sitting in the attic, not sure what had just happened. Cleo had barely opened an eye, and Tortuga was sprawled out on the rug, aimlessly flapping her legs in the air.

"Out of the way!" Moki shouted. "King Tut's on the bridge!"

"Also known as Mask Face or Mac 'n' Cheese," Rani added, her pink sari hiked up.

The puzzled adults leaped to their feet and followed. Sergeant Dan was out the door first. The cups of coffee resting on their laps somehow miraculously escaped crashing to the floor.

It only took seconds for the kids to realize they had been outsmarted once again by the taunting masquerader, who had quickly retreated across the bridge and disappeared into the dark woods bordering the zoo and park. Moki's dad forbade them from following.

The twins' dog, not one to follow anyone's orders, kept up the chase. His disobedience paid off when he returned a short time later, dragging something that bumped noisily across the bridge's wooden slats. The four kids ran forward to inspect his prize.

It was Mask Face's death mask! Inside was a label. Sergeant Dan beamed his flashlight on it. Moki gasped. Then he read out loud, "Ancient Sands Curio Shop."

# CHAPTER EIGHT

· ✦ ·

# Cactusville Clues

B etween yesterday's incident at the reptile house and the spooky activity on the Quince Street Footbridge, the squad was happy to see daylight again. The twins' tutor Bruce Wilding zipped along the highway in his blue classic Mustang convertible with his four detective passengers. They had for the most part brought him up to date on their case.

"So, tell me again why I'm driving you kids out to the sweltering desert this hot afternoon," Bruce asked. "Just because I teach you during the week doesn't mean I have to be your chauffeur, you know. It's Sunday. This is supposed to be my day off."

"We're all glad you're back from San Francisco," replied Lanny. "But living with us comes with obligations, like letting us look cool in your car." Bruce glanced in the rearview mirror and caught a glint in the boy's eyes. "And we want to follow up on some things Dr. Abbott and Dr. Kurtz told us about the mummified Egyptian cobra. There have been some problems at the reptile gardens regarding their snakes and venom supply. I thought if we went out to Cactusville, maybe we'd get some valuable info and pick up some leads."

"Just so we don't pick up any snakes," Moki said, raising his hands high to catch the wind.

"What Moki's really saying, Bruce, is that he wants your services as a bodyguard today, too," Lexi said, elbowing Moki next to her in the back seat.

"Being your bodyguard was not what I was hired for, but it often seems to be necessary. You four have gotten into more than your share of scrapes in your travels and adventures."

"That's right, Lexi," said Rani. "Remember last year when Bruce pulled both of us at the same time out of that bog in the Yucatan jungle when we were on vacation down there?"

"Yeah, it's because he has such big arm muscles—for an old guy." Lexi high-fived Rani.

"Old guy? You call twenty-five old? With any luck, you'll get there yourselves someday," Bruce replied, not taking his eyes off the road. "And I emphasize the words *with any luck*."

"If you'd been on the footbridge with us last night, maybe we all could have chased Mask Face into the woods," Rani said. "And maybe that crazy person would be in custody right now."

Before Bruce could reply, Lexi said, "Moki, my dog

wasn't too happy when your father took his prized find away last night."

"Dad said maybe the crime lab could get some evidence from the mask that could lead to its owner. It was pretty funny, though—a dog named Pharaoh dragging a pharaoh's mask. Maybe he wanted to be crowned King of the Nile Dogs." Moki reached across Lexi, chuckled, and high-fived Lanny.

"Good ol' Pharaoh!" Rani said from the ever-popular front passenger's seat. "He got some great evidence for us. That mask label practically screamed 'Augusta Ramsey.'"

"What I want to find out is how did Mask Face know we were in our office? And why did that nut try to scare us again?" Moki asked.

"I hate to break it to you four, but you're already world famous despite being new, amateur detectives here in town," the tawny-haired tutor stated. "People know where you live. All it takes is for one person to know your office is in the attic, and the word gets around. Plus, I'll bet your light was on up there last night."

"Yeah, and Mask Face could've been trying to warn us not to help Mrs. T," replied Lanny. "That stunt had the opposite effect on me, however." The boy looked up at the bright blue sky, smiled, closed his eyes, and enjoyed the feel of the intense desert sunshine on his face. The pungent aroma of desert sage mingled with every air molecule.

Moki noticed Lanny's blissful look. "Pretty different

scene now from last night in the dark with those snakes, huh, bro?"

"Yeah, bro," Lanny answered quietly as Bruce entered the Reptile Gardens' parking lot.

"Wow. Nice car," said a visitor, who had just pulled in next to them. "What year?" the man asked, not taking his eyes off the vehicle as he circled it, scanning every detail.

"It's a '67," Bruce said, beaming. At this point, all four kids jumped out and leaned against the car with their arms and legs crossed, basking in the glow that came from being associated with Bruce's cool vehicle. "In case you kids haven't noticed, we're here," Bruce said, popping their dreamy bubble of self-absorption. "Get over yourselves and come on," he said, attempting to hide his own proud smile as he led the group toward the crowded entrance.

"What's everyone want to do?" Rani asked once they were inside the park grounds.

"It's noon now," said Bruce in his take-charge manner. "I suggest we all meet back over there at the Ssssso Delicioussssss Café for a late lunch at two." He pointed right. "Twins, your parents want you home by four-thirty to help with dinner, so we need to be back on the road by three-thirty."

Moki declared that he was having as little to do with snakes as possible, so he headed off to the tortoise enclosure while Bruce strolled to the nature art gallery. Lanny, Lexi, and Rani hurried to the venomous snake show that was about to start. Many other visitors had the same idea.

"Hmm. 'Cobras Off Exhibit Today,'" Lanny read out loud from the sign posted in front of the arena. "That matches with what Dr. Kurtz told Moki and me about those snakes being shipped off to the zoo."

"Darn, I was looking forward to seeing the handlers interact with the cobras," Rani said.

"Speaking of that, I've always wanted to ask you— and since Moki isn't around—did you ever have any close calls with cobras or other snakes when you lived in India?" Lanny asked.

"My whole family did once. I was five. That was right before we moved to Las Palmitas. A king cobra got into our house one hot summer night, probably from the veranda. It must have wanted to escape the heat. Anyway, cobras smell like skunks. We smelled something bad and searched but couldn't find it. So we just sat down to dinner. Big mistake. It was definitely in the house because soon, the skunk smell got stronger. Turns out it had crawled right under our big dining room table and—get ready for this— smack across my mom's feet! She played it really cool, telling all of us not to move a muscle. We knew that meant the snake was there. Well, thank goodness, after what seemed like an hour, we finally saw it crawl away into the living room, where it coiled itself around the base of a large flower pot. My dad ran for the local snake catcher who captured it in a cloth sack and took it away. What a night! The snake was small, only about six feet long."

"Whoa," Lexi replied, grabbing her friend's arm too tightly. "I'm surprised *you're* not the one who's afraid of snakes."

"Snakes were part of our life there," Rani said, peeling Lexi's hands off herself. "I found them fascinating. I also remember we always had to watch for them when we were in the garden or if we walked through tall grass. But don't tell Moki. He'll probably freak and not even want to be around me—you know, death by association or something. Seriously, though, you can't really blame him for his fear. He didn't grow up with snakes as I did. And we tend to be afraid of what we don't understand."

"Don't worry. I won't be the one to tell him," said Lanny, then added, "If I'd known you liked snakes, I would have asked you instead of Moki to go with me to the zoo yesterday," he added with a wink.

"And I would have accepted, too," Rani quickly replied, steadily meeting Lanny's gaze.

Lanny cleared his throat and continued, "So, uh, instead of the show, let's go over to the cobras' glass enclosures and see if we can learn anything about them, even if they aren't there. Maybe there's some information posted that will be important to our case," he said, inspecting his copy of the park map. "They should be over that way." He pointed directly ahead.

The three kids made their way to the Reptile House and, as expected, found two empty cobra enclosures side by side: the king cobra's and the Egyptian cobra's.

"That enclosure must have been Wadjet's," Lexi said as she pointed toward the Egyptian cobra's empty space for the snake now at the zoo. "Yup. There's her name above the pen."

"Wow, this is interesting," said Rani. "It says on the sign here, 'The king cobra that lives in India and Southeast Asia is only a distant cousin of the Egyptian cobra that lives in Africa. As a result, the two venoms have some similar chemical components but also some very important differences. The king cobra's venom is so lethal that one dose can kill ten people or an elephant.' But get this. 'The Egyptian cobra's venom is actually stronger.'" Rani glanced up at her friends.

"Some different chemical components, huh?" Lanny said. "That's interesting and adds to some info Dr. Kurtz shared with Moki and me. Let's try to find out why the cobras are off-exhibit. Maybe we can find somebody who will tell us." He scanned the area for anyone in charge.

Meanwhile, Moki's and Bruce's paths had crossed by the prairie dog community mound. The two stopped for several minutes and watched the little critters scurrying around, wrestling with one another and searching for food.

"Look at that one," Moki said. He pointed to an older prairie dog. "He must be the boss. Look at how he's trying to protect some of the younger ones from some of the bullies. Well, Bruce, at least you've never had to rescue me," Moki said, remembering the conversation they'd had during the drive. "I think I'm too big and too careful to ever need your bodyguard services."

"I hope you're right. I'm not that much bigger than you." Bruce looked Moki over.

The tutor decided to take a few photos of the cute animals before moving on. Moki's attention was drawn to a small child who had started crying by the enclosure behind him.

"What's wrong, little girl?" he asked. He walked over and squatted down to her level.

"I dropped my teddy bear into the big lizards' cage," she replied with her fists rubbing her eyes. "Can you get it out for me? I love Teddy. Please, please help!"

Moki looked over the cement sides into the large, grass-covered enclosure. The stuffed toy would be an easy reach for him since it had landed on a ledge instead of on the floor of the pen. Three giant Komodo dragons roamed at some distance inside, swishing their heavy bodies and tails side to side as they crawled. One had already spotted the toy and was lumbering toward it.

"Sure, little girl. No problem. Hawaiians know all about rescuing teddy bears but mainly from inside volcanoes," he teased. Moki eyed the approaching dragon warily but stood up as tall as possible, bending forward from the waist over the edge of the enclosure to reach the toy. It was three feet below. Behind him, he heard rapidly scuffling feet coming his way. Before he knew it, Moki felt a tremendous push on his shoulder. He was hurled head first into the pen!

The little girl's mother screamed, which brought Bruce running. Whoever had shoved Moki maneuvered nimbly through the crowd, escaping before the tutor could get a fix on the attacker.

"Moki!" Bruce called.

But Moki seemed to have been stunned by the fall. One of the Komodo dragons was closing in. No helpful zookeepers were in sight, and there was no time to lose. Bruce vaulted into the pen four feet down, grabbed Moki's arm, and propelled him toward the enclosure's wall. Moki, regaining his senses, realized his predicament and clambered over the side, somehow managing to snag the stuffed toy on his way out. His rescuer was right behind him. The two escaped with only seconds to spare. A disappointed dragon stared up at his would-be meals with an open but empty mouth. The onlookers applauded.

"I was almost a Hawaiian appetizer for a big lizard," Moki said, using one hand to calm his racing heart and the other to hand the little girl her toy. "The final *alo-HA*," he said breathlessly.

As the crowd disbursed, the two caught their breath. "Now, what were you saying about not needing me to rescue you?" Bruce asked. Moki looked at Bruce, and the two burst out laughing.

Then Bruce grew serious and pulled Moki over to a nearby water spigot. "You picked up some dragon saliva on your arm from the enclosure. Better wash it off. Komodo dragons have venom sacs in their mouths." Cold water flooded over his arm and hand, and the goo disappeared.

"Didn't know that. Thanks again. Reptiles, ugh!" Moki said, shaking off the water droplets.

Lanny, Lexi, and Rani arrived at the café to find Bruce and a disheveled, still damp Moki waiting. Bruce held open the restaurant's glass door, and a blast of refreshing, cold air greeted them.

After a waitress showed the group to a booth, the guys explained to their friends what had happened to them. The three listeners' mouths dropped open.

"The little girl's mother said the person who pushed Moki was a man with a small build, in his late forties or early fifties. She said he deliberately ran at Moki." Bruce took a small bottle of hand sanitizer from his pocket and used it before reaching for a menu.

"It certainly sounds as if it was done on purpose," Lexi replied. "But thanks so much for rescuing our courageous Moki, Bruce. In fact, I'd say we have two heroes among us today—Moki and Bruce. So, I won't ever tease you again about being our bodyguard because you just proved that you definitely are." She reached over and squeezed his muscular arm.

"I'm sure you'll never tease me again," he said, trying to disengage Lexi's vice-like grip. "At least not until the next time. But it had a happy ending, so let's eat. I'm starved." He passed the hand sanitizer around the table, then gave the menu his full attention.

"Yeah, I'd rather eat than be eaten," Moki laughed, giving Lexi a sweet wink.

During lunch, the group discussed more about Moki's attacker. "Does anyone besides me see any similarities between the person who pushed Moki and our forever-disappearing Mask Face?" Rani asked as she cleaned ketchup off her bangles.

"Well, they both win the award for speed and agility," Lanny said, downing some greasy fries.

"Bingo," Rani said. "Plus, they're the same small size, and Moki's attacker is a man."

"So, if Moki's attacker was actually Mask Face, then we know it's a 'he.' And he must have followed us out here from town," Lexi said after a big gulp of her iced tea. "Stalker. Creepy."

"Remember, we need evidence of identities and motives before we can say with certainty that we're now dealing with one person, not two," Lanny said. Lexi scrunched up her nose at him.

"Which reminds me, we should check out Augusta Ramsey tomorrow," Moki said.

"Yeah, let's do that right after seeing how Mrs. T's doing," Lanny replied.

Bruce set down his dessert fork and asked, "Did you three get any clues or leads yourselves?"

"We overheard two herpetology assistants talking about the snakes and venom that are being held temporarily at our zoo," Lanny answered. "It seems an investigation is underway into the recent disappearance of some of this park's cobra venom. If the missing venom isn't connected to our current case, maybe it's another mystery we can tackle later."

"Yeah, but again, as long as we aren't tackling any snakes," Moki said, glaring at Lanny.

After lunch, Rani suggested that they make a quick stop in the gift shop. Time permitted, so the group entered the tiny store packed with souvenir buyers. Looking straight ahead, the squad received another shock. Standing at the check-out counter purchasing plaster cobra statues was Dr. Granger's business associate and Ancient Sands Curio Shop owner, Augusta Ramsey.

# CHAPTER NINE

· ✧ ·

# The Egyptian Pond

The kids gazed at the refreshing, shimmering pond Dr. Thornsley had built in his backyard just last summer. They could never get enough of it. It was especially inviting today after yesterday's heat and adventures in Cactusville. The pond was rectangular: twelve feet wide side to side, five feet back toward the fence, and two feet deep. The below-ground grainy concrete structure was a haven for dozens of sparkling goldfish and colorful lotuses. Lexi had named it, "The Egyptian Pond."

They were also mesmerized by the pond's raised stage that continued to the whitewashed concrete wall, five more feet back. It evoked an ancient temple by the Nile with its palm trees in large pots, some feathery papyrus plants, and a tall stone obelisk carved with hieroglyphics. In the center were large ornate urns from which grew snake ferns, pungent jasmine, and white and blue lilies of the Nile. On the left front of the stage was a four-foot-tall statue of the jackal-headed god, Anubis. On the right was the bird-headed god, Horus, Lexi's personal favorite.

At the front center of the temple stage and extending forward on its own concrete slab a foot out over the pond was the most captivating object of all—a four-foot-long, reclining stone sphinx. It was an exact, though miniature, replica of the Sphinx of Giza that has guarded the pyramids in the Egyptian desert for millennia. Like the original, part of its nose and a chunk of its headdress were missing. Every bit of the pond's planning and construction had been lovingly overseen by Dr. Thornsley, whose presence Lexi thought could certainly be felt as strongly here as in his study.

Tortuga rested on the pond's grainy lip. Rani often brought her to this spot to soak up some sun and snag bugs. The morning's sunlight dappled the tortoise and the still water. Being a tortoise, the pet preferred drinking the pond's water to swimming in it. Though she was known to take an occasional, accidental plunge, so the kids watched out for her. Mrs. Thornsley always enjoyed hearing about how Tortuga had "helped" the four detectives on some of their previous cases.

"Remember the time when Tortuga found a sapphire ring on the lawn over on Tamarind Street?" Moki asked. The others nodded. He smiled, stroked Tortuga's bumpy shell, and offered her a red hibiscus flower from a nearby bush. Tortuga wasn't one to turn down a treat and gobbled it in rapid bites.

"She does seem to have an incredible nose—and mouth—for objects," Rani replied proudly. She eyed her amazing pet as it made short work of Moki's offering.

"Yeah, and I remember how she bit that one burglar's hand when he was snooping around in Rani's backyard one night," Lexi said, glancing at her friend. "Boy, did he get a big surprise."

"I'm certain you're all remarkable detectives, including Tortuga," Mrs. Thornsley said. "So, kids, have you noticed anything different about the pond since the earthquake?" She glanced mainly at Lanny though her large sun hat partially hid her face.

"Now that you mention it, there are some cracks on and around the statues," the boy replied. He climbed up on the stage for a closer inspection. "Some detectives we are— lost in Tortoise Land while that damage was staring us right in the face." Lanny straightened up and looked at his friends.

"This morning I conducted an earthquake inspection myself around the property," said Mrs. Thornsley. "I found those statue cracks, so I called Mr. Bailey to come over and check the pond as well. He's the mason who worked with my husband last year to design and install the pond and its statues." Her hands were clasped tightly as she sighed in remembrance of happier times.

At that moment, the front doorbell rang, jarring the woman back to the present. "That must be Mr. Bailey now." She cleared her throat and excused herself to answer it.

She soon returned to the yard with the mason. "Sam Bailey, Seeds Sow Fine Gardeners," they read on the emblem attached to his dark green uniform.

"Mr. Bailey, these are Las Palmitas's four world-famous detectives. I'm sure you've heard of them," said the widow, motioning to the kids and introducing each by name.

"Hello. Yes, I saw you on the Internet," the middle-aged mason replied, barely looking up as he busied himself by rummaging in his tote bag for a clipboard, pencil, and some measuring tools. He walked toward the pond. "Don't worry, Mrs. Thornsley. I'll do a thorough inspection, and we'll make everything right as rain if need be."

Moki decided to take the tortoise from the pond's edge and place her on the grass for her safety while the mason worked. Nonetheless, Tortuga instantly made a bee-line for the man.

"Whoa there, turtle. I'm not too fond of reptiles," Mr. Bailey said, quickly jumping onto the stage next to the statue of the god Anubis.

"Actually, she's a desert tortoise, California's official state reptile," Rani said. "Don't worry. Just ignore her, and she won't bother you." The strategy worked, and Tortuga eventually lumbered off to munch on the thick grass in the exotic, organic garden.

"Well, Mrs. Thornsley," said Mr. Bailey, looking up from his task some minutes later. "I'm sorry to say there is definitely earthquake damage to these statues, mostly to the sphinx. Everything else looks fine. I do recommend that we fix the problems. Unfortunately, I have lots of inspections in the next few days due to the tremor, so I can't start the repairs until next week. You'll be first on the list, however." His smile and a handshake sealed his promise, and Mrs. Thornsley showed him out to his truck.

Once the woman returned, the twins and Moki set to their real purpose of the day's visit by filling her in on what Dr. Abbott had told them recently. They shared only a few clues and theories they had already developed, not wanting to burden her with too much information until they had some solid evidence to report. Meanwhile, Rani wandered over to the pond stage to inspect the statues herself.

"Oh, I'm so relieved to hear Dr. Abbott believes my late husband to be innocent and that he's supporting all your efforts," said Mrs. Thornsley. She happily lifted a large watering can to douse the pond stage's plants. Lexi and Lanny helped. Soon, Rani joined in the chore.

Moki was keeping an eye on Tortuga for her safety. As if she noticed him watching, the tortoise plodded toward him from the side of the pond where Mr. Bailey had been standing. She was clasping something beige in her mouth, which caught the boy's attention.

"Tortuga, bring it here, girl," said Moki, tamping the ground in front of himself to get her attention. "Don't eat it!" He held out a geranium flower, hoping she would find it more captivating.

His strategy worked. Tortuga obeyed him and allowed Moki to take a slightly gnawed slip of paper from her mouth in exchange for the treat.

"Good girl, Tortuga. Hmm . . . It looks like a sales receipt for a meal at Shady's Lunch Shack. And it's dated yesterday," he read. This caused the others to turn toward him. "Is this yours, Mrs. T?" he asked, walking over and handing the rumpled slip to her.

"No, I don't know that restaurant. Mr. Bailey must have dropped it." She handed it back.

Moki pulled out his phone and entered the restaurant's name and address. "It shows here the café is just off the Desert County Highway," he told the group.

"Desert County? That's only about ten miles north of Cactusville," Lanny replied.

Next, Moki entered "Desert County." "There isn't much out in Desert County except a large natron pit and last-chance gas stations and cafés," he said, looking up at the others.

"Maybe gardeners and masons use natron in their work," said Mrs. Thornsley.

Rani had rejoined the group and had her phone out, entering "natron." "Well, let's see. It says here, 'natron is a mixture of sodium carbonate decahydrate.'" She read slowly to pronounce each word correctly. "The natron in Desert County is 'a modern kind, being hydrated soda ash and minerals.' It doesn't mention any gardening or masonry uses," she said, scrolling down the page.

"I'm reading that too, and this is interesting," Moki said. "There's a valley of naturally occurring natron in Egypt that has been there for thousands of years called, *Wadi El Natrun*. It was the type of natron used in ancient Egyptian burial rituals for mummifying bodies. Wouldn't there be natron inside the stolen urn since it contains a mummified cobra?"

Uncharacteristically, Lanny wasn't listening. His favorite pond had once again cast its spell, transporting him back in time to ancient Egypt. He sat at its edge in an almost hypnotic state.

"Hey, Pond-Boy," Moki said, having approached his friend. No response. "Hey, *Pond-Boy!*" he said closer to Lanny's ear while shaking the boy's shoulder.

This time Lanny looked up, and the others, including Mrs. Thornsley, started laughing.

"Yeah, I'm talking to you," Moki said. "The girls and I are ready to leave. We're going to Ancient Sands Curio Shop next, remember? Seems to me you've been to 'Ancient Somewhere Else.'" Moki grabbed Lanny's arm and began lifting him onto his feet.

"Sure, whatever you say, *Honu-Kāne*," said Lanny, pushing Moki's hand away and staggering to his feet on his own.

"Well, now we all know there's definitely a good reason why the name *Lanyon* in Cornish means 'a cold pool of water'!" Moki joked, slapping Pond-Boy on the back.

"Don't make me even sorrier I shared that piece of

info with you in a weak moment, bro," Lanny replied, punching Moki's bare, tanned arm with some force. "And by the way, in Cornish, *Lanyon* also means 'St. John's Church.'" Moki smirked and returned the punch.

"You're being little boys. Stop it," Rani said. She cast a pathetic look at them, then at Lexi as the boys backed away from one another, smiling. She returned Tortuga to her towel-lined box in the little red wagon the girl used to wheel her pet around town.

Moki rallied to his responsibility and took the handle. He always preferred to be the chauffeur of the tortoise taxi. Mrs. Thornsley said her good-byes to the pet.

Rani then turned to the twins and said quietly, "Speaking of 'weak,' I was asking my dad the other day what kind of damage our earthquake might do. He said the recent earthquake wasn't that bad, that it would really only damage weak or poorly built structures."

"Like the Egyptian pond statues?" Lexi asked with her eyes wide open.

"Yeah, like the 'weak or poorly built' Egyptian pond statues," she replied.

# CHAPTER TEN

· ✧ ·

# Curious Curios

It was a short bicycle ride from Mrs. Thornsley's Nutmeg Street house to Jacaranda Street. Entering Ancient Sands Curio Shop was like taking a time machine back to antiquity to witness a sacred ritual. A dusky stillness and natural light enveloped the place, compelling the four kids to hold their breaths and lower their voices.

"It feels like a spooky, old tomb in here," Moki whispered. "I think Ms. Ramsey should have named this place 'Ancient Dust' instead of 'Ancient Sands.'" For a change, he dexterously avoided upsetting a display on a grimy, cluttered table top.

"Well, I can see why Dr. Granger wants to use some of these objects for the festival exhibit. They do look realistic," remarked Lanny. He ran his finger over a statue of the cat goddess Bast.

The place had no other customers, and no one had come out to help them yet. Just then, Lexi remembered some important news she hadn't yet shared with her friends. "You guys," she whispered. "I almost forgot. This morning before Lanny came down for breakfast, I was telling Uncle Rocky about seeing Augusta Ramsey in Cactusville. He told me that late yesterday afternoon, when he and his girlfriend Angie had stopped at Grounds for a Cup Coffee House on the Boardwalk, in walked, guess who?—Augusta Ramsey." Lexi was almost dancing in front of her tightly-grouped friends.

"Cool it, Lexi. We don't want to attract the wrong kind of attention," Lanny said. "Question. How does Uncle Rocky know her?" He glanced around to ensure a still-empty shop.

"That's what I asked him. He said he's seen her often since they both shop at the Feed Bag Grocery Store right across the street from here. But here's the interesting part. He also said that in the coffee shop, she joined a man already seated, and they talked for half an hour."

"Wow. Busy lady. Who was the man?" Rani asked, now also scanning for eavesdroppers.

"Uncle Rocky didn't know, but his description of the man matched Dr. Granger perfectly," Lexi said, bringing her voice back to a whisper.

"But wait. Doesn't Uncle Rocky know Dr. Granger on sight since the guy works with your parents at the ARC?" asked Moki with a dog-tilt head.

"Uncle Rocky and Dr. Granger have never met. Dr. G's never been to our house," Lexi said.

"Okay. I'll grant you Dr. Granger and Ms. Ramsey meeting over coffee is interesting," said Lanny. "But remember. They're working on the ARC exhibit together. Maybe they had more to discuss about that."

"But on a Sunday and outside of either of their workplaces? Smells fishy to me," Lexi replied, sticking up her nose at her too-logical brother.

"If you think those two are in cahoots . . . that means up to no good together," replied Lanny, "you'll need some solid evidence." By now, his hands were on his hips in his don't-mess-with-me stance.

Moki intervened. "Oh, no. Is this going to be another vocabulary-building day?" He banged the heel of his hand on his forehead. "But, no good this time, bro. I already know what your word means."

Rani quickly added, "Well, Mr. Lanny the Linguist, from the mask, we have some fairly solid evidence that Ms. Ramsey and Mask Face have met. Maybe more of those masks are here. Let's look. Anyway, we'd better split up and move around before anyone gets suspicious."

The four did just that and started looking at the displays. Many of the curios were replicas of valuable artifacts and treasures, mostly from ancient Egypt. Lexi thought she recognized a few of the objects as those Augusta Ramsey had just purchased in the gift shop in Cactusville. There were also several gold-painted funeral masks encrusted with fake jewels and many sizes of statues of numerous ancient Egyptian deities scattered around the shop. There was an entire section devoted to furnishings such as ornate chairs and gold-plated settees befitting a pharaoh or queen. Against the walls were tall, plastic date palm trees and Styrofoam pyramids in various sizes.

"*Alo-HA*, come check these out," Moki said proudly, motioning quickly to the other three. The four did a double-take on duplicates of the very mask worn by Mask Face! The girls quickly clasped their hands over their mouths to stop a barrage of shouts. Lanny high-fived Moki.

"There's your evidence, oh brother of mine. The mask," Lexi responded with a smirk.

"And there's that mac 'n' cheese taste again I get with the word 'mask,'" Rani said.

The most amazing curio, however, was a seven-foot-tall, beautifully painted, coiled plaster Egyptian cobra with its hood expanded in warning. It leered menacingly at the shop visitors from a dark corner to the left of the back office. While gazing at it, Moki could feel the hair on the back of his neck standing on edge. He tried his best to compose himself between shivers.

Lanny was thinking that with just the right imagination, a person could visualize they were on a movie set, and Uncle Rocky's favorite actress, the violet-eyed Liz Taylor, was about to appear for her next scene as Cleopatra, Queen of the Nile. Instead, the bird-like proprietress, Augusta Ramsey, emerged from behind an ornate purple and gold curtain that served as her office door.

"Oh, it's you—I mean, hello," Ms. Ramsey said with

a shaky voice and furrowed eyebrows, eyeing the four kids collectively. "What can I do for you?"

"I'm looking for a book on ancient Egyptian hiero-glyphics," Lexi replied flatly. True—if only partly.

"I have some on the table over there. The rest of you, feel free to look around," she said with her eyes roving from one face to the next.

"You have some great objects here. I understand you will be using some of them for the ARC's festival exhibit," Lanny probed.

"Yes, that's the plan. But how did you know that? You're one of the Wyatt twins, aren't you?" Ms. Ramsey asked. Lanny couldn't help but hear a tinge of smugness in the woman's voice.

"To answer your first question, Dr. Abbott told us when we saw you in the lobby of the ARC the other afternoon. Remember? And to answer your second question, yes, I am one of the Wyatt twins. This is my sister, Lexi, and over there are our friends, Rani and Moki," Lanny said, standing tall. "You were talking with Dr. Granger at the ARC as I recall," Lanny pushed.

"Yes, I remember you," she snapped, not offering any further information, but Lanny thought he detected a flash in her bird-like eyes. "Excuse me. I have some business in my back office. Ring the bell on the counter when you're ready to make a purchase." Augusta Ramsey turned and made a very hurried exit from her four persistent customers.

"Seems to me she couldn't wait to get away from us," Moki whispered.

"Seems to me she can't wait to get rid of us," replied Rani.

The four kids put a strategy into play that Lanny had learned from watching spy movies—stalling for time while wandering around the premises. They were hoping Ms. Ramsey would reappear so they could ask her some more questions. They also suspected the longer they stayed in the shop, the more nervous she might become, which might make her slip and reveal some valuable information. Perhaps about the masks or Dr. Granger.

The detectives separated with Moki and Rani moving over by a table filled with more masks and jewelry. Lexi and Lanny used up some time combing through the pile of dusty books on ancient civilizations near the office door.

"Check this out, Lanny," Lexi said, holding out a colorful book for her brother to see. "Here are the hieroglyphs of Menes and Wadjet that Dr. Abbott showed us the other day."

"Yeah, I recognize them . . ." Lanny replied, gazing at the picture.

But before he could finish his sentence, the twins heard an odd scraping sound coming from behind them. As they turned to see what was causing it, they spotted the gigantic plaster cobra from the recesses of the shadowy corner, toppling toward them.

# CHAPTER ELEVEN

· ✧ ·

# Alley Spy

When the twins regained their senses, they found themselves against the shop wall in a dusty heap, with Moki and Rani on top of them and shattered plaster all around them.

"What happened?" demanded a somewhat dazed Lexi, rubbing her arm. "Oww, you're crushing my leg."

"Sorry." Rani climbed off her, and the four rose from the floor. "I saw that thing falling, and all I could think to do was tackle you."

Augusta Ramsey emerged from the back room. Seeing the four kids standing and apparently unharmed, she looked astounded. "What have you done to my shop?" she blurted.

The dust was clearing, and the mess was revealed in full. The cobra had been huge. Who knows how injured they would have been had Rani and Moki not knocked them out of the way? And for once, they couldn't blame Moki for the disaster.

"Yes, we're fine. Thanks for asking," Lexi said through pinched lips.

The shop had not fared as well as the kids. Surveying the damage, they saw the formerly sinister-looking cobra broken into hundreds of harmless plaster pieces scattered across the floor. A few displays had been smashed, including the book table the twins had been rummaging through only a few seconds before the crash.

Lanny wasn't so controlled for a change. "Your statue nearly killed us!" he barked at Ms. Ramsey. "And don't start telling us that we knocked it over because we never touched it."

"I never accused you of anything, young man. You need to leave now. I've got to clean up this mess." With her hands on her hips, Augusta Ramsey's black-clothed arms looked like raised raven wings.

"Okay, we'll go, but only if you tell us . . ." Lanny jabbed his finger toward the table with the Mask Face masks. "Has anyone bought one of these masks recently?"

"What?" The woman's face clearly paled. "Ye—no! Why would you even ask—no, I don't care why. Just leave."

"But—"

"I said leave!" She now looked like a bird of prey about to take serious flight at their faces.

The four left the store without another word, still brushing plaster dust off themselves while heading for their bicycles locked to the lamppost in front of the shop.

"I'd say Ms. Ramsey just implicated herself in our

case," Lanny stated with some satisfaction. "I thought she was going to faint when I asked about the mask."

Moki caught Lanny's arm as the girls continued walking. "Bro, remember the other night when we were locked in with the snakes, and we were talking about crushes? Well, what just happened with that plaster monster back there gives a whole new meaning to the word 'crush.'"

"You said it, bro," replied Lanny, slapping Moki on the back. "Let's get out of here."

The four kids had only gotten a few yards away from Ancient Sands when they noticed a man up ahead clearly glaring at them from around the corner of a passageway that led into the alley.

As soon as they noticed him, he bolted into the alley behind Ancient Sands and its neighboring shops.

This time, Lanny led the spontaneous pursuit. They moved as fast as they could pedal, but the stranger was too crafty. He disappeared from view, ducking between two buildings where they couldn't ride. They quickly jumped off their bikes to follow on foot, but he was long gone.

"Well, that was random. Did anybody get a good look at him?" Lanny asked as they retraced their steps to claim their dropped bikes.

Rani sighed and said, "No. His hair and face were hidden by his baseball cap. But you know what? I had that mac 'n' cheese taste again, now with this alley guy."

"But he wasn't wearing a mask," Lexi said. "Is your synesthesia telling us that Mask Face and this alley runner are the same person?"

"Whoa. Slow down, Lexi," Lanny replied. "That's quite a stretch. But I'm curious, Rani. Do you know if any crimes have ever been solved by synesthetes using their special abilities?"

"Hmm, I don't know, but if not, there's always a first time," she said with a twinkle.

"Yeah," Moki added, still catching his breath, "and we could add that to our business cards. 'Cases solved by skill, strength, good looks, and extrasensory brain power.'"

"You guys are too much," Lanny said with a head shake. "Let's get back to what we know. First, the alley runner is a *he*. Second, I think what's safe to assume is this guy wasn't Dr. Granger since he is much shorter and skinnier than the Egyptologist."

"I think it's also safe to assume Augusta Ramsey wants us out of the way, and I agree we need to rethink who that man is—in addition to being her accomplice, that is," Lexi said. "The accident in the shop and now this? These aren't just coincidences."

"I'll take it a step farther," Rani said. "I'll bet he was hiding in her office, helped her push the cobra over onto you two to scare us off the case, then sneaked out the back door to spy on us," Rani said, pointing to the shop's back door leading into the alley. "And here we have—or should

NUTMEG STREET: EGYPTIAN SECRETS

I say had—another great runner, mask or no mask."

"You're right, at least about the 'great runner' part," Lanny replied, still brushing himself off. "And Lexi, you might be on to something about the two events not being coincidences."

"*Might be?*" his sister asked incredulously, staring at Lanny and slapping her hand to her forehead as if her brother was zany. "Wait. I know. We need evidence, right?"

"Right. But let's head for home. I've had enough danger for one day, and we've picked up some good clues. Besides, we can get this disgusting cobra plaster dust off ourselves."

"Here's a clue I picked up," said Moki. Everyone stopped in their tracks and gave him their full attention. "Even fake snakes can be dangerous."

The others punched him playfully on the arms, and Lexi pulled his cap down over his eyes. Moki was content to leave it on the bridge of his nose for the moment for dramatic effect.

"Now, you can't see anything, let alone snakes," she said.

Lanny quickly changed the subject. "Hey, bro, you and I have a meeting this afternoon in your backyard with a large basket of fruit, don't we?"

"Sure thing, bruddah," Moki replied with a huge smile.

Lexi and Rani looked at each other and rolled their eyes at the boys' mysterious appointment as the friends mounted their bicycles for the seven-block ride back to Quince Street.

A short time later, the four kids entered the twins' kitchen to find Uncle Rocky and Pharaoh. The cook was finishing his lunch while Pharaoh danced around impatiently for some bits of food to fall in his direction.

"Can I interest you four in some delicious, gooey peanut butter and jelly sandwiches and tall glasses of ice-cold milk? Hey, you look as if you took a dust bath," the cook said. He scanned them up and down. For a few seconds, he forgot about his lunch invitation. "Where have you guys been?"

The kids told him the events of the morning, from the cracked statues in Mrs. Thornsley's garden to the incidents in Augusta Ramsey's shop and alley. Uncle Rocky had set his last bite of sandwich down and listened closely with wrinkled brows.

"I have four comments," said the cook. "Number one, I'm very glad you weren't hurt. Number two, we should call the police, or at least Sergeant Dan, and report this. Number three, this morning, I saw Ms. Ramsey talking with a different man from yesterday. And, number four, go brush yourselves off on the patio before you mess up my clean kitchen." He pointed to the back door. But the kids' eyes lit up as they focused only on Uncle Rocky's third comment.

"Uncle Rocky, tell us what you saw," Lexi pushed, jumping up and down while gripping his arm. "Where were you when this happened? Who was the man with her? What were they doing?"

"Okay, Missy, one question at a time, please, and don't rub my arm raw," Uncle Rocky said, trying to peel away her hands. "I'll just tell you the story. If I leave anything out, then you can ask. Early this morning, I went out to do a little grocery shopping at The Feed Bag Grocery Store on Jacaranda Street. The store is right across the street from Ancient Sands, you know. It must have been before you four got there because as I was leaving the grocery store, I noticed Augusta Ramsey standing out in front of her shop talking with a man. She handed him two small packages. Then he followed her into her shop. You don't have to ask—no, I didn't recognize the man, but I can tell you whoever he was, he's small in build, has dark hair, and was glancing around like a suspicious character." The cook then popped the last bite of his sandwich into his mouth. "Sorry, Pharaoh. All gone." He patted the dog's head.

"Package Man's build sounds like Mask Face's and Alley Spy's," Moki said. He never got tired of creating clever names for their suspects. Actually, the other three counted on his talent.

"That's great information, Uncle Rocky," Lanny said.

"So, who are your main suspects so far?" the man asked as he refilled Moki's milk glass.

"Augusta Ramsey, for sure," Lexi said between sandwich bites. "Maybe Dr. Granger."

"And Mask Face, given that the mask came from Ms. Ramsey's shop," Rani replied.

Lanny added, "Others as well. We can only call them 'Persons of Interest' for now since we're missing the necessary evidence. Moki, correct me if I get their names wrong—Dragon Pit Man from Cactusville, Alley Spy from just now, and Package Man, who got something from Augusta Ramsey earlier this morning as Uncle Rocky just reported."

Moki nodded.

Rani said, "What links most of these Persons of Interest and Mask Face is their running skills."

Moki added, "And their small builds." Then he downed his second glass of milk.

"And their zany behaviors. Don't forget those," Rani replied. "I wonder what was in the two packages Ms. Ramsey gave Package Man," she said, chomping on a carrot stick.

"Well, whatever it was, it must have been valuable because Augusta Ramsey appeared to be lecturing Package Man about them and didn't look as if she trusted him with whatever the contents were." Uncle Rocky set out a plate of fresh peach slices for dessert.

"It could have just been some items the man had bought at her shop, and she wanted him to handle them carefully," Moki said as he popped two slices of fruit into his mouth.

"Moki, you're beginning to sound too much like my logical brother," Lexi replied with a glare. "No more lunch for you." She pulled the fruit plate toward herself and Rani.

"I don't think it was about shop purchases," Uncle Rocky said quickly. "They acted like they knew each other really well."

Lanny said, "Okay, if there isn't anything else, I say we've had enough for one day. Thanks for lunch, Uncle Rocky, and for the super clues. Now, time for some fun after our near miss with the plaster cobra. You girls might want to watch what's about to happen."

The squad headed out into the twins' backyard. Moki and his dad lived around the block on Palm Street and directly behind the twins. The two families conveniently shared a back fence in which they had installed a gate soon after the Kalanis moved in. Moki led the way through the Wyatt-Marlton's fragrant flower garden and the gate, then through his own yard teeming with tropical plants. He opened the sliding glass door to his house, and they entered the Kalanis' kitchen.

Without warning, the two boys started jumping around as if they were kindergartners going on a field trip. The girls stared at this highly unusual behavior and exchanged worried glances.

They were soon distracted by loud squawks. It was Moki's talking pet mynah bird, Aloha. "*Aloha*, what's bakin'? Aloha *akamai*. Aloha *no ka oi*!" he chattered, hopping from perch to perch in his enormous cage. The newspapers underneath it were littered with seed hulls and punctured orange peels.

"What did Aloha just say?" Lexi asked, offering the bird a sunflower seed.

"He said that he's 'smart' and 'the best.' The other day after the earthquake, he said, 'What's shakin'?' Then after the Snake House episode, it was 'What's snakin'?' Now, it's 'What's bakin'?' I think Aloha knows Lanny and I have plans for some old fruit. My dad and I think we should have named the bird 'Nostradamus' instead."

"So, just what are you two going to do with the fruit?" Lexi asked. "Bake an apple pie?"

"Watch and see, my little *ku'uipo*," said Moki, smiling and chucking her chin. "It's an idea we brought to life from a computer game."

Moki ran upstairs and returned shortly with two old, extra-long t-shirts and a very real *katana*, or sheathed Samurai sword. The girls were all eyes. "My uncle sent it to me from Japan," he said, ensuring the girls could see his tanned, flexed arm muscles as he raised the heavy sword.

Lanny and Moki donned the t-shirts, tied black sashes across their foreheads, and put on thick garden gloves. Then they grabbed the sword and fruit basket from the kitchen counter, and all four headed for the backyard compost pile. Once there, Moki hoisted the *katana*, and Lanny took the pitcher's position several yards away.

"We call this 'Chop-chop Composters,'" stated Lanny. "Watch!"

Lanny proceeded to take a rotten mango from the basket and pitch it at Moki, who whacked it as hard as he could with the *katana*. Both screamed boisterously with each successful hit. Fruit bits flew everywhere, including all over the guys and the corner fence. The girls barely managed to escape being covered with juice and fragments. After a while, the boys switched places.

"And Mom and Dad let you do this?" Lexi asked. Her eyebrows raised.

"Sure, why not?" Lanny replied, positioning the sword. "The fruit's rotten, after all."

After watching this chaos for a few more minutes from a safer distance, Lexi turned to Rani and exclaimed, "Boys! Why is it we're so much more mature than they are?"

"I don't know why, but thankfully we just are," replied Rani, glancing back at the action.

"I have a great idea. I don't know about you, but I'm ready for something more civilized," Lexi said with both hands on Rani's shoulders. "Let's go make tea. I think Uncle Rocky has some of his delicious frosted brownies with sprinkles left over from Saturday night's dinner, too. And you can tell me more snake stories from India and about the custom of women getting henna tattoos for various ceremonies."

"You're on, BFF," Rani replied with a smile and a high-five.

The girls turned away from the boys, who were having too much fun to notice let alone remember their crushes had ever been there.

"Ta-ta, Philistines," Lexi said, making a face over her shoulder.

"Yeah, ta-ta, Barbarians," Rani added, spinning back around toward the fence.

Both dashed through the gate, not bothering to close it, gladly leaving the oblivious boys to their joyous, messy chopping.

# CHAPTER TWELVE

· ✧ ·

# Midnight Pond Prowler

The morning after the plaster-cobra scare, the heat returned, and a sultry wind gusted steadily through the mullioned windows in the twins' third floor classroom on Quince Street. It sent the sheer curtains billowing straight into the room. The day's lessons had just ended.

"Okay, so let's get this mess cleaned up," Bruce said to the two. Despite the hefty breeze, clay, paint, and paste odors permeated the room.

"Bruce, you're a great teacher," Lexi said as she helped gather paste jars. "You make learning fun because you always come up with interesting ways to present things."

"A compliment? So, what do you want from me this time?" the grinning tutor asked.

"Nothing, really. I meant what I said," the girl replied. "And without you, we'd have to stay home and go to regular school when our parents travel around the world for their jobs. I'd rather travel with them and have your school-on-the-go."

"Yeah," her brother added, tossing newspapers into the recycle can. "If we stayed home, we'd not only miss all that traveling, but we'd also have fewer mysteries to solve. I'll take your traveling school over regular school any day. Plus, with you, we get your awesome car."

Bruce knew they were right about his job. He had accepted the position as their full-time tutor in order to travel and be with the interesting Wyatt-Marlton family. It beat working in a walled-in classroom, and the pay was better than what the local school district offered.

"Lanny and I like learning from you even if you make us do summer school three times a week," Lexi said. "Oh, and by the way, how about a ride to the beach in your Mustang with the top down this afternoon?"

Bruce's reply was cut off by Rani and Moki's arrival. They had been directed to the upstairs classroom by Uncle Rocky. "*Aloha*, everyone," Moki said, as he strode toward the group.

"What did we miss today?" Rani asked. She picked up a small pot with a *papier-mâché* falcon's head. "What's this? Looks like something out of ancient Egypt."

"It is," replied Lexi, taking the object from her friend. "This falcon represents Qebehsenuf, protector and carrier of what's in the pot." She lifted the lid to reveal a blob of pinkish-red paste. Pushing it under Rani's nose, she said, "A pharaoh's intestines! Bruce has been teaching us about the ancient Egyptian mummification process. The priests in charge of mummification used four Canopic jars, which were buried with the pharaoh. Each jar contained the viscera, or internal organs, of the dead ruler. Sorry for the vocabulary lesson. I know I'm sounding like Lanny. Anyway, the second jar—"

But Lanny cut her off. "The second Canopic jar with Duamatef, the jackal-headed god, guarded the stomach."

Lexi elbowed Lanny aside. "I'll take over. After all, I'm the future Egyptologist." She held up the last two jars. "This one with the baboon's head is Hapy containing the lungs. And the one with the woman's head is Imsety holding the liver. See?" Lexi and Lanny showed their two friends the contents of the other jars, each containing the appropriately colored mound of paste.

"Ugh! Sorry I asked," Rani said, gagging. "That doesn't go at all well with a hot day and the scrambled eggs I had for breakfast." She fanned her face with both hands, hoping for some fresh air.

"Then I'll leave out the part about how the high priests pulled the brains out in chunks with hooks through the nostrils because the ancient Egyptians didn't think the brain was as important as the other organs," replied Lexi. She pushed Imsety's jar into Rani's ashen face again. Her friend pushed it back.

"Natron was very important in the mummification process," added Lanny to stop his sister, "because it was a dry preservative. It worked with the arid climate to help dehydrate the pharaoh's embalmed body, so it could be wrapped in linen bandages, then entombed for its journey to the afterlife." He showed his friends a scoop of a white sandy substance Bruce had used.

"Stop. Where's the jar for the heart?" Moki asked.

Lanny replied, "The heart of the soul was left in the body. It had to be weighed by Anubis, the god of the dead, to see if it was lighter than the Feather of Truth. If it was, it could enter the eternal paradise of the Field of Reeds. The person had to have done good deeds during his or her lifetime to make the heart light."

Lexi quickly added, "But if it was heavier than the feather, the heart was thrown to the ground and devoured by Amut, the crocodile-faced god. Good-bye, immortality."

"Wow," Rani said. "Paid to be nice. Still does."

"So why was the mummified cobra put into an urn instead of a Canopic jar?" Moki asked.

Bruce replied, "Canopic jars came into use later during the Old Kingdom, about 4,000 years ago, long after your mummified cobra. Plus, those jars were reserved for pharaohs' internal organs. Still, that must have been one important snake. Okay, enough for today. We'll be back here in two days when we'll discuss ancient Egyptian hieroglyphics. Rani and Moki, you're invited, too. Oh, by the way, kids, your parents want me to keep a close watch on you after that plaster-cobra incident yesterday, even though—let's be very clear—I'm not your bodyguard."

"That sounds to me like more chauffeuring for us."

Lanny smiled at his friends. "No need to twist my arm to take a ride in your souped-up Mustang."

"Speaking of arms, your muscles sure are big, Bruce," Lexi said. She and Rani exchanged looks and snickered.

"It's 'surely,' not 'sure,' and all the better to protect you guys, even if I'm not your bodyguard," he said. He neatened his desktop and put some pens into the desk drawer.

"Yeah, and I bet your girlfriend Katie likes them, too," replied Lexi. She and Rani burst into laughter.

Once again, Bruce's reply was cut off. Uncle Rocky's raspy voice drifted up from the kitchen. "Hey, twins, Mrs. T's on the landline. It sounds like she has a problem. Come running!"

The four friends and Bruce dashed down two flights of back stairs. Lanny arrived first and took the phone receiver from Uncle Rocky's outstretched hand. "Hello, Mrs. T. This is Lanny. I mean, Lanyon," he said with a soft voice, hoping Moki, the teaser, wouldn't hear him use his real name. After listening carefully, he said, "Don't worry, Mrs. T. You did the right thing. We'll be there in a few minutes to help investigate. We're only three streets away," and he hung up.

Turning to the group, he said, "Guys, Mrs. T saw a moving light and heard tapping sounds by the Egyptian pond around midnight last night when she got up to open her bedroom window. She called down, but the person ran off. The police came last night, but they've just returned to do more investigating. She wants us to come over as well."

"Let's go right now," replied Rani. "Poor Mrs. T. What's next?"

Bruce said, "Since the police are over there, you can go on your own. But remember what your parents said, twins. I want to know before you leave Mrs. Thornsley's where you four are going." Bruce emphasized his admonishment with firmly planted hands on hips.

"I second that idea," Uncle Rocky said and put his hands on his hips, too.

"Wow, I guess we have no choice, squad. Okay, we'll call in," Lanny said.

Their word was always good. Once they had been reminded, that is.

The four kids found Sergeant Dan and two other police officers in Mrs. Thornsley's yard. Law enforcement had just finished combing the area for evidence. The kids hugged the widow and asked how she was doing. After she assured them she was better, she showed the kids a small fresh footprint to the left of the pond's stage. Sergeant Dan's squad of police officers was taking photos of it and the area.

Lanny walked around to face the pond and rapidly noticed the statues' cracks were bigger than he had remembered them following the earthquake. But the most startling revelation came when he stared at the sphinx. He called out loudly to his three friends, "Come check this out! Do you remember the cracks in the sphinx's paws being that big the other day?" Lanny pointed to the large fissures in the statue.

"They're definitely bigger now," Lexi replied.

"But this amount of damage doesn't match with what my dad said to expect from the earthquake we just had," added Rani with a puzzled grin.

"Mrs. T, what's the sphinx made of?" Moki asked, turning to the woman.

"It's plaster with a sandstone coating to make it look authentic. But it's hollow in its thickest areas," she replied.

"Well, if it has some hollow areas, maybe it could sustain this kind of damage, but that still doesn't explain how or why the cracks suddenly got deeper," Rani said with a frown.

"Are any of you thinking what I'm thinking?" Moki asked. "That the midnight prowler is responsible for enlarging the cracks?" He leaned down and picked a floating leaf from the pond.

"Yes, I think that's a good working theory," Lanny replied, "and it would explain the tapping sounds Mrs. T heard. But as to why someone would do that, it's a mystery to me."

Moki turned to his dad, who was nearby. "Dad, did you or your assistants find anything else that might be important to our investigation—anything at all?"

"Possibly. What do you kids make of this?" Sergeant

Dan held out a small plastic evidence bag containing a dirty, wrinkled business card. "I found it to the right of the pond stage."

Moki read aloud, "'Mr. Buster Hobart, Hobart's Pond Pad, Ginkgo Street.' Who's that?"

"He's the man who cleans the pond and keeps it stocked with lotuses and fish," Mrs. Thornsley replied. She was happy to have so many experts present.

"Has he been here lately, Mrs. T?" Lexi asked. The woman shook her head.

"Well, it could be a definite clue to the prowler's identity, or else it's possibly just a plant," said Lexi.

"A 'plant'?" Moki asked, cocking his head. "Looks more like a business card to me."

"That's detective talk for evidence left purposely at a crime scene to give a false clue so as to lead law enforcement officials or detectives in the wrong direction," Lanny replied.

"That's good thinking, kids," Sergeant Dan said, handing the bag to his partner. "We'll check with Mr. Hobart in the next few days to see what we can learn."

Moki looked at Lanny. "Bro," he whispered, "let's break the rules and beat them to it."

"Yeah, let's go see Mr. Hobart ourselves. Then you could report our findings to your dad." Lanny rarely let his devilish side reign. The team usually got better results when he acted maturely. This time, however, he wanted to get a lead. Heading to Ginkgo Street was the right next step.

The boys joined the girls and the officers by the pond. The police agreed the cracks in the sphinx's paws looked as if they had been deliberately made with a chisel and hammer, probably by the prowler and not as a result of the earthquake. As to the prowler's motive, they didn't have any theories, either. An officer dusted the area for fingerprints.

Sergeant Dan said, "That prowler knew what they were doing and probably wore gloves. By the way, the crime lab found only some dark-colored human hair in that pharaoh's mask the twins' dog retrieved from the park last Saturday night. Maybe that will help you kids."

"Thanks, Dad. Now we know Mask Face has dark hair just like Package Man. Of course, maybe it's just a coincidence," Moki added quickly, observing the logical detective Lanny's gaze.

"Okay, Mrs. Thornsley. I think we've done all we can do here," Sergeant Dan said. "Be sure your side gate is locked tonight. I'll have a patrol car cruise by several times this evening." He and the other officers headed for their cars with Mrs. Thornsley escorting them out, offering her thanks.

The girls liked Moki and Lanny's idea about going to question Mr. Hobart right away. "Darn! We have to check in with Bruce first," Lexi said, kicking at the grass.

"Hey, look at it this way. It's a free ride in a cool car on a hot day," Lanny replied, nudging his twin's shoulder. "Maybe Brainy Bruce the Bodyguard won't be so bad to have around after all. I'll text him right now. Bet he replies 'yes' to Hobart's."

"Now it's my turn for a fabulous idea—if I do say so myself," Rani said. "How about if we ask Mrs. T if we can spend the night here with her? She'll feel more protected. Then, after she's gone to bed, we can set up a stakeout just in case that prowler decides to return. Maybe they didn't finish what they set out to do. After all, Mrs. T did scare the person away after hearing the tapping. With any luck, we just might catch the prowler."

The others thought it was a great idea. When Mrs. Thornsley returned, they told her their idea of staying to protect her and the pond, conveniently not elaborating on the stakeout part.

"That's very sweet of you kids. Yes, I would like that as long as you don't take any risks and your parents give their permission. I was starting to feel afraid about being here alone tonight, especially as the police drove away."

"Never fear. We'll be here," Lanny replied. "We'll come back around eight tonight with our sleeping bags. We can camp out in your living room if that's all right with you."

Smiling, Mrs. Thornsley said, "Now, don't forget to get permission. I'll chaperone and have the living room floor ready for you. And definitely some dessert, too."

Moki, the Cookie Man, turned and gave her a wink and a big hug.

# CHAPTER THIRTEEN

· ✧ ·

# Pond Watch

The kids had only gotten a short distance from Mrs. Thornsley's when they saw Bruce pulling over to the curb. "Glad you called," the tutor said. "Get in. I'll drive you to Hobart's Pond Pad. It's too hot to walk seven hills down to Ginkgo Street. Besides, I think I know the owner from a class we took together at the university." He jumped out quickly to pop the convertible top.

Lexi could already feel the sizzling sidewalk penetrating her flip-flops and agreed with her brother that a breezy ride in Bruce's cool car would work out just fine. They all dashed to the blue Mustang and piled in after the usual debate about who got to ride shotgun.

"Will you teach me how to drive your fab car someday, Bruce?" asked Lexi as she started to slide over to see what it felt like to sit in the driver's seat.

"Someday, maybe, but for right now, the best seat in this car still belongs to me, so scoot over." He started to nudge her, but Lexi got the message and moved to her spot, expertly missing, from experience, the floor-mounted gearshift.

As he drove, Bruce asked for an update about what the police found at Mrs. Thornsley's that necessitated the four kids spending the night there and why they had to go to the pond shop now.

"Just don't take any unnecessary chances at Mrs. Thornsley's tonight," he said. "And if Hobart's the same guy I remember from college, then I doubt he'll turn out to be one of your suspects."

"Why do you say that?" Lanny asked while waving to a friend he spied strolling down the street.

"Well, I remember him as a really nice guy. We were lab partners in a tough chemistry class. But Hobart loved it. In fact, he got his degree in chemistry. If it hadn't been for all his brains and help, I might have flunked that course." None of the kids could imagine Bruce ever coming close to flunking any class.

The group soon arrived at the pond shop. Indoors was cool and refreshing. Filtered light danced playfully over plastic pools containing a myriad of colorful lotuses and varieties of tropical fish. The place had the feel and subdued scent of a pet shop, minus the barking and chirping.

"Well, Bruce Wilding, right?" said Buster Hobart. The man strode toward the tutor and offered him a robust handshake.

"Hey, it *is* you," Bruce replied, clasping his hand.

NUTMEG STREET: EGYPTIAN SECRETS

"Nice shop, Buster. I'm sure there's a chemistry set around here somewhere."

"Sure thing. It's in my office. Comes in handy in this business."

Bruce introduced the tall, long-haired man to the four kids. The shopkeeper shook hands with each of them and explained how chemistry was important when he tested pond water for his clients. It ensured their ponds were habitable for particular aquatic fish and plants.

"What would make a pond uninhabitable?" Lexi asked. She gazed at a nearby pool of fish.

"Many things, especially harmful substances like herbicides, pesticides, toxins, and high concentrations of chlorine."

"And you can test for all of those?" she asked.

"Well, sometimes I get assistance on the toxins from Dr. Kurtz at the zoo. She's a great person and an expert on toxins, especially since she's the curator of herpetology," Buster replied.

"We know her," replied Moki flatly. "But we've just come from Mrs. Thornsley's."

"It's so sad about her husband. He was a very honest and intelligent man. His death was such a loss. We talked a lot when I serviced his pond. I do miss him."

"That's why we're here, Mr. Hobart," Rani said, getting right to the point. "The police found your business card by the Thornsleys' Egyptian pond this morning and wondered how it got there." With the toe of her shoe, she gently pushed up some of the shop floor's sawdust.

"Gosh, that's strange. I haven't been there since before the doctor passed away." He stared at his feet for a few seconds. Then looking up, he asked, "May I see the card?" He held out his hand.

"Uh, we don't have it," Lanny replied. "The police do. There was a prowler by the pond last night, so they took it as possible evidence." He watched for Buster's reaction.

"Well," began the shopkeeper, scratching his head, "if I need an alibi, I was at a late movie with some friends last night. Oh, and here's one of my current business cards. Did that card look like this?" He presented Lexi with one of his cards from a holder at the check-out counter.

"Actually, no, it didn't," Lexi replied. "The other one was old and very dirty and not even the same design." She described the card in detail.

"Ahh, that was the type I used last summer."

Lexi continued, "Have you worked with anyone from Seeds Sow Fine Gardeners or Ancient Sands Curio Shop? We know the gardening company helped build Dr. and Mrs. Thornsley's pond."

Buster Hobart crossed his arms over his chest. "No one at Ancient Sands. I do occasionally work with those gardeners, however. Their mason Sam Bailey and I collaborated on the building of that pond about a year ago. Mr. Bailey had just come to California from somewhere in the Midwest. I helped him break into the business here in

Las Palmitas. He seemed like a decent enough guy though he was somewhat quiet as I remember—as if he had a lot on his mind."

"Is there anything else you can remember about him? Anything at all?" Moki asked.

"Well, now that you mention it, he seemed pretty shy, so I mainly dealt with the Thornsleys when it came to planning and installing the statues. Basically, Sam talked to them through me."

"Well, thanks for all the interesting information, Mr. Hobart. This is a terrific shop," Lanny said, sweeping his gaze around the place.

"Thanks, and come back anytime," he replied. The group worked its way to the front door. "Buster, good luck with your business," Bruce said, shaking hands with the man again.

"Wait," Lexi said, stopping at one of the pools. "I want to buy a lotus for Mrs. T and the Egyptian pond." Since blue was her favorite color, she picked out an exotic blue-violet bloom, which Mr. Hobart prepared for transport home. Then he thanked them again and saw them out.

On the drive back to Quince Street, Moki said, "Mr. Hobart seemed very friendly and gave us some valuable information." The boy tilted his head back to sun his already tanned face.

"He doesn't seem the type to jeopardize a job he enjoys so much by committing a crime," Rani replied. "Plus, he has an alibi for last night." She waved to a friend walking up the street, hoping it would earn her "cool points" for being spotted in the front seat of Bruce's classic car.

"Maybe," Lanny said. "We could check his alibi to be thorough."

"As I said," Lexi replied, staring at her brother, "his old business card was probably a plant after all." She drummed her fingers impatiently on top of the front leather car seat.

"When I get home, I'll let my dad know Mr. Hobart's business card probably isn't a direct lead to the prowler," Moki said. He closed his eyes against the sun. "Where to next, bro?"

"We should go see Mr. Bailey at the garden shop," Lanny replied. He donned his sunglasses.

"It's late afternoon and hot. You should save Mr. Bailey for another day," Bruce replied. Then he grinned and continued, "Besides, you four are going to Mrs. Thornsley's tonight to . . . uh . . . 'keep her company,' right?"

"Right," Lanny said emphatically while avoiding Bruce's glance in the rearview mirror.

As much as the kids wanted to continue their investigation, they had to admit Bruce's thinking about postponing a visit to Mr. Bailey was practical. Glimmers of adventures ahead and the idea of possibly nabbing the prowler this evening at the pond pacified them for the time being. Before long, the car wound up the curved driveway on Quince Street. Everyone piled out and thanked Bruce for the ride in his cool car before heading indoors.

The time approached when each detective would have to get parent permission for the sleep-over that night. Lanny knew it had to be done truthfully yet carefully so as not to ring any alarm bells with the adults. They had earned a mutual respect with their parents because of their maturity and habitual trustworthiness. He had no intention of jeopardizing that trust. Lanny spent some time convincing himself there was no real danger in their pond stakeout plan. After all, the four of them would be together at all times at Mrs. Thornsley's, and she would chaperone. Those kinds of rationales had sufficed for the adults in the past. The boy hoped this time would be no exception.

"Lexi, how thoughtful of you," Mrs. Thornsley said that evening as she placed the lotus with the other exquisite blooms floating on the surface of the pond. The kids had arrived promptly at eight with sleeping bags tucked under their arms. Darkness was closing in, and an enormous summer full moon was already rising, imparting a bluish, fairylike glow to the garden and the pond.

"Come into the living room and pick out your sleeping spots," Mrs. Thornsley said. "Then, help yourselves to some homemade chocolate cake. It's all ready for you on the dining room table."

"Mrs. T, how did you know I like cake just as much as cookies?" Moki asked.

"Oh, something just told me that would be the case," she replied as she stifled a chuckle.

The girls set up camp under the grand piano. The boys took spots in front of the fireplace.

"Good thing we chose the piano first," Lexi said to Rani. "Moki would've bumped his head on it if he had to get up quickly in the middle of the night."

"I heard that. Ha, ha," Moki replied as he threw his overnight things toward the hearth.

The evening went quickly. By nine, the group had long finished their dessert, and Mrs. Thornsley announced she was going to bed. "I didn't get much sleep last night because of that prowler. I know I'll sleep much better tonight with you four here. I'll come down later and check on you. Thanks so much, and enjoy your slumber party."

"We will, Mrs. T," Lanny replied and craned his body to watch her climb the stairs to her room. As soon as she was out of sight, he turned to his friends and said, "We'll take shifts staying awake."

Lanny heard Mrs. Thornsley's footsteps in her bedroom directly over the living room and continued, "Okay, squad. Let's get ready to crack this case wide open. We already decided to stand our shifts outside in the garden. Good thing we all wore dark clothing, what with that bright moonlight. Moki, you and Lexi stand the first two-hour watch. Rani and I will rest until you come get us. We'll repeat that system until dawn, if necessary." He handed each one a flashlight he pulled from his backpack.

"I just hope the prowler shows up," Lexi replied. "We need a break in our case."

"I just hope Mrs. T doesn't, or she might find us on a stakeout," Rani added, biting her lower lip.

"I don't think she will," said Moki. "Too tired."

Moki and Lexi very quietly made their way out into the side garden through the dining room's French doors. Moki hid behind some hydrangea bushes to the left of the pond. Lexi took up her post in a mass of papyrus to the right of the pond. As minutes passed, her imagination, the strong scent of night-blooming jasmine, and the scene carried her far away. She imagined herself an Egyptologist in the moonlit Egyptian desert, thinking about the day's frustrations and successes she and her crew of diggers had experienced, and planning the work for the next arduous day ahead. At that make-believe moment, Lexi became overwhelmed with how very eternal Egypt actually felt. Here she was, gazing at the same moon ancient pharaohs and queens had observed from their palaces in the desert sands millennia ago. Just before an imaginary caravan of camels plodded past the camp in her head, she was jolted back to reality by a touch.

"Hey, my little Egyptian princess, it's eleven. Our watch is over. Let's go wake up the second shift, *wiki-wiki!*" whispered Moki. He took her hand and led Lexi quickly on tiptoes indoors.

"How did you know what I was dreaming about?" Lexi asked, stopping short inside.

"We Hawaiians are all-knowing and intuitive," Moki replied without missing a beat and grabbing another piece of cake as they passed the dining room table.

The watch shifts continued as scheduled all night. No prowler. And Moki was correct. No downstairs visit from a soundly sleeping Mrs. Thornsley.

All at once, around five a.m., the yard's cricket serenades abruptly ended, and Lanny and Rani heard a distinct rustling sound. It was coming from the papyrus on the right side of the pond. The two were on alert as they watched from their posts. Lanny looked around for something to use in case he had to subdue the prowler, then remembered the heavy flashlight in his hand. That would do the trick, he decided. *Get ready to pounce*, he told himself.

Just then an opossum mama emerged from the papyrus. She was leading her babies back to their canyon home after a night of successful foraging.

As Lanny slinked into the house mumbling under his breath, Rani grabbed his arm, batted her eyelashes at him, smiled, and asked, "Isn't being a detective such an exciting, glamorous job?"

# CHAPTER FOURTEEN

· ✧ ·

# Red, White, and a Blue Sedan

The Cortez Park Bell Tower east of the house was already chiming twelve o'clock when the twins stumbled down the back staircase and into the kitchen. Everyone had let them sleep in late after last night's "slumber party" at Mrs. Thornsley's. Bruce was long gone to his summer enrichment class but told Uncle Rocky he'd be home by one, and the kids were to wait for him before going anywhere.

Lexi rubbed her eyes and inhaled deeply. "I smell rain in the air," she said sleepily.

"Good morning—I mean, good afternoon," replied Uncle Rocky. "A big rainstorm is expected this evening, but it might not wait that long." He had just squeezed fresh orange juice for the sleepyheads.

Angry gray clouds already knifed across the sky, occasionally cutting out the sun and gaining momentum for tonight's deluge. The oppressively hot air created a sense of ominous expectancy. Even the usually gossipy crows that congregated in the side yard's orchid tree each afternoon were oddly quiet, casting their wary eyes upward. The early summer storm could, however, provide welcome relief from the recent heat and humidity that were uncharacteristic of late June in Las Palmitas.

There was a single knock at the back door and in sauntered Rani and Moki, also appearing a bit bedraggled after the long night. "We all look about as wide awake as Cleo over there in the corner," Moki said sarcastically. The cat was in full sleep mode on her back with floppy paws extending upward at unnatural angles, resembling a large, dead cockroach.

The cook greeted the new arrivals and handed them some juice. Then, he quickly returned to his much-loved pastime, watching his favorite cooking show, *Cuisine with Marceline,* on the wall-mounted kitchen television.

"Uncle Rocky, you don't need to watch that show," Lanny said, having emptied his glass. "You're a fabulous cook already."

"Me? I'm just a chow jockey. Marceline is, well, she's . . . the 'Cuisine Queen,'" the cook crooned while glancing at the ceiling. "I get some great recipes and cooking tips from her. Plus, she's a gorgeous lady."

"Watch out, Uncle Rocky, or Angie will get jealous," snapped Lexi. She glanced at Rani.

"No way. Angie's for real and a swell girlfriend. Best of all, she's right here in town." He sighed, "Marceline is in faraway France. By the way, Bruce will be home soon, and you're to wait for him to take you wherever you're planning to go. As soon as Marceline says, '*Au revoir*,' I'll pack you five a big picnic lunch for your travels—or maybe it should be brunch since you twins didn't even have breakfast."

"Thanks, Uncle Rocky. Lunch will do. You're so sweet," said Lexi.

Once he began preparing the food, the smiling cook let the four kids regale him with tales of last night's opossum stroll on Nutmeg Street. "You didn't take any risks last night, did you?"

"Us? Take risks? Never with opossums," Lexi replied. She fluttered her eyelashes at him.

"Hmm . . . Instead of Lanny, I think *I* should give you kids a definition starting with the word 'risks'," he said. His chopping knife was poised in midair.

"Hey, guys," said Lanny, trying desperately to change the subject, "it's so muggy, and rain isn't due for hours. Let's postpone our visit to Mr. Bailey and head to Mango Beach instead."

"Yeah, and it'd be fun to see how Boardwalk Boulevard's been decorated for next week's Fourth of July celebration," said Rani. She popped a grape into her mouth from the fruit bowl.

They knew Bruce would be willing to go. The tutor came home just as Uncle Rocky finished packing the lunch basket. The four kids had already put on their swim gear and gotten their surfboards. After a long, hot morning in class, Bruce was very ready for a dip in the ocean himself.

The five soon arrived at Mango Beach. The boulevard shops were elaborately festooned with patriotic bunting and signs for the Fourth. Red, white, and blue flags and lights were strung from one palm tree to the next lining the beach. The group captured the last parking place close by and loaded themselves down with their beach gear and lunch basket. Soon, they found a sandy spot with a patch of blessed shade, courtesy of some sizable palm fronds that dipped toward the sand.

Bruce watched from their beach camp as the four kids thoroughly enjoyed themselves surfing in the dark blue water of the Pacific Ocean. It was obvious Moki had been born to it, having trained on the tall, sometimes treacherous Hawaiian waves on Oʻahu's North Shore where he had won a few competitive surfing trophies in the years before moving to California.

All five devoured the picnic lunch while the kids spent time summing up the current clues and suspects. Augusta Ramsey and Mask Face topped the list, followed by Dr. Granger and maybe Mr. Bailey. "Mom and Dad told me the other day they actually heard Dr. Granger say something complimentary about Dr. T recently," Lexi said, biting into a sandy peach.

"Well, that's good to hear, and about time," Moki replied between cookie bites. "Maybe he isn't involved in the theft at all. We haven't seen him out anywhere, lately."

"True, but I'm not ready to cross him off our list yet, bro," said Lanny. "Maybe he and Ms. Ramsey really were just talking about the festival exhibit when Uncle Rocky and Angie saw them together in the coffee house, but maybe not." He grabbed more pretzels to satisfy his salt cravings.

"Well, let's definitely see Sam Bailey tomorrow," Rani said. "Other than Mask Face and all our Persons of Interest—you know, Dragon Pit Man, Alley Spy, Package Man, and now Pond Prowler Person—we haven't interviewed Mr. Bailey except very briefly at Mrs. T's the other day."

"And I'm wondering about what Mr. Hobart said—that Mr. Bailey was so shy he couldn't even talk to Dr. and Mrs. T," said Moki before chugalugging some icy fruit punch.

"I thought that was strange, too," Lexi replied. She deposited her peach pit into the group's portable trash bag. "Being shy isn't exactly a trait someone in business would want to have. On the other hand, maybe he was unsure of himself because he'd just moved to Las Palmitas."

"You know, Mr. Bailey didn't seem to have any trouble talking to Mrs. T the other day," said Rani. She had applied more sunscreen and was now putting some on Lexi's back.

"Maybe he's gotten over his problem. After all, it was a year ago Mr. Hobart worked with Mr. Bailey on the Egyptian pond," Lanny reminded them.

"I'm for trying to find out tomorrow," Moki said, stretching out on the warm sand.

The kids' let's-run-it-down discussion was soon interrupted when the rainstorm abruptly threatened to arrive ahead of schedule. The clouds had scared away the sun, wind noisily swooshed the palm fronds, and a few raindrops splashed the beachgoers. Bruce suggested they pack up fast and head to the car for home. But not before stopping at Moo Cow's Dairy Town shop a few blocks away for their traditional, after-beach ice cream cones, Moki reminded him.

As Bruce collected a few stray towels from their beach spot, the four detectives, with arms loaded, made it to the parking lot. They stopped to admire more palm tree holiday decorations when Lexi suddenly screamed. She swung her board at the others, knocking Rani and Lanny down and causing Moki to jump backward, away from her and the road. A speeding sedan roared by, missing them by inches, then zoomed out of the lot. Their beach gear was scattered everywhere.

"That same blue car again!" Moki yelled, racing off behind it. But he had no chance to catch up with the vehicle. He returned to the group, all back on their feet again and thanking Lexi for saving their lives. "No license plate that I could see. Just like before," Moki reported.

"Did you get a look at the driver?" Lanny asked. "Did anyone?"

Heads shook all around, but the other three thought it had to have been Mask Face.

"All I saw was a gigantic beach hat, no head or face," Rani replied, stomping the ground. "And no mac 'n' cheese flavor, but maybe that's because we were in the danger zone."

About that time, Bruce caught up with the group. He had witnessed the near-accident from the beach.

"Come on! Let's follow that nut," he growled, bounding for his car. "Boardwalk Boulevard's busy this time of day, so maybe he's stuck in some traffic up ahead. It's worth a try, anyway."

The kids stowed their gear in record time and easily vaulted into the convertible Mustang without opening the doors. Bruce backed out of the parking spot but was immediately trapped by other cars pulling out ahead and behind him. Apparently, they weren't the only ones eager to outrace the storm.

"Let's run after him," Moki said and started climbing out of the car.

"No way, Moki," Bruce replied, grabbing his arm. "We don't know where he is. It's too dangerous, and I'm not in the mood to rescue you again." All they could do was sit in the snarl and picture the blue sedan somehow magically disappearing up Boardwalk Boulevard, traffic or no traffic. For the second time, the sedan driver—very likely Mask Face—seemed to have the kind of luck they lacked. Moki promised Bruce and the squad he would report the incident to his dad.

"Ice cream, anyone?" the tutor offered again after the

traffic eased. "We could use something to make us forget our failed attempt." The kids didn't have to be asked a third time.

"Yeah, a pineapple-coconut sherbet cone for me—two scoops," Moki replied.

The car pulled into Moo Cow's. Everyone got their favorite flavor and discussed Mask Face, agreeing they must be doing pretty well on the case to make the driver so obviously desperate. Even Lanny had to agree with that supposition.

No sooner had Bruce dropped his passengers off at their homes and gotten his car under cover when the sinister clouds ripped open. The storm lashed the streets and trees mercilessly.

Rain drummed on the roof and beat against the windowpanes all night, lulling the Quince Street family into a sound sleep. Not that the previous night's pond watchers and this afternoon's stalking victims needed any help.

# CHAPTER FIFTEEN

· ✧ ·

# Disaster and Discovery

The next morning dawned much cooler with blue skies, marshmallow clouds, and crisp air. The entire revitalized Quince Street household was up early. Drs. Wyatt and Marlton had bicycled to the ARC, and the twins were just finishing their lesson on hieroglyphics with Bruce in their upstairs classroom. Pharaoh and Cleo were chasing each other's tails, clattering indiscriminately around the first floor rooms. They kicked up dust and left some small Persian rugs in heaps.

"Nutty pets," muttered Uncle Rocky to himself as he cleaned up the kitchen from breakfast. "More work for me, compliments of their royal majesties—make that their royal stinkers!"

Upstairs, Lexi said, "Bruce, I think I've mastered drawing the hieroglyphs for Menes and Wadjet." She held up her work for Bruce to check. The tutor had been teaching the twins the hieroglyphs that represented the major ancient

Egyptian pharaohs, queens, gods, and goddesses.

"I'd say you have—" he began, but Uncle Rocky's frantic shouting interrupted him.

"Kids, come running! Mrs. T's on the landline again, and she's very upset, more than the other day."

"Oh, no. I hope nothing's happened to Mrs. T or the pond," Lanny said as he slammed down his work and started for the door. "Maybe last night's storm did some damage."

Once again, the twins and Bruce sailed down the back staircases two steps at a time with Lexi reaching the phone in Uncle Rocky's outstretched arm first.

"Mrs. T, this is Lexi, I mean Alexia. . . . Oh, try not to cry. Tell me what's happened."

Lexi listened for a long time, uttering an occasional, "Uh, huh," and "Oh no!" until Lanny, Bruce, and Uncle Rocky thought they would scream from impatience. Finally, Lexi told Mrs. Thornsley they'd be there in a few minutes and hung up.

"You just aren't going to believe this," Lexi began with catches in her voice, "but when Mrs. T went outdoors this morning to check for storm damage, she found the stone sphinx even more hacked up and all the pond life dead." The girl fought back tears and hugged herself.

Bruce replied, "Rocky, will you please call Rani and Moki and ask them to meet us at Mrs. T's, pronto? Come on, twins. Head to my car." He gently pushed them toward the back door.

"Sure thing. Consider it done," the cook answered solemnly, already starting to make the first call.

In a few minutes, the twins and Bruce reached Nutmeg Street and found Moki and Rani just stepping onto Mrs. Thornsley's front porch. The widow was watching for them and frantically yanked opened the door.

"Oh, that rascal," she said, wringing her hands. "He must have come back last night and destroyed the pond. Too bad you kids hadn't spent the night here again. No storm could have done this much damage, and we haven't had any more earthquakes." Mrs. Thornsley started to cry. "He must have taken advantage of the storm's noise. I slept right though his shenanigans."

"Let's all go take a look together," Lanny said, fidgeting. Lexi embraced Mrs. Thornsley.

Nothing could have prepared the group for what met their eyes. The formerly beautiful pond they all loved was indeed lifeless. Dozens of fish were floating on the water's surface, and every lotus, including the one Lexi had recently bought, was withered.

Lexi gasped at the site. First, Dr. Thornsley died. Now, his cherished pond. It was too much. She covered her face with her hands and started to cry. Rani cradled her friend in her arms, allowing her own tears to flow. Lanny, Moki, and Bruce were frozen, speechless.

Almost more startling was the sphinx. Its paws had

deeper grooves in them, and again, they appeared to have been deliberately made. Everyone agreed the major damage had to have been the work of a person, not merely nature.

Bruce recovered from the catastrophe first and said, "Since the police haven't been called yet, I suggest we do that immediately and notify Buster Hobart, too. Perhaps he can help determine what killed the pond life."

"And nobody touch anything near the pond until the police arrive," Moki reminded them.

Mrs. Thornsley had recuperated sufficiently to call the police herself, requesting Sergeant Dan to come if he was available. Next, Bruce called Buster. Both men were expected soon.

"Why do strange things keep happening around my house since my husband died?" the widow asked. Her knuckles were white from gripping the back of a patio chair. "Are these things connected to him or the urn's theft somehow? I wish I understood." The woman burst into tears.

"We'll figure it out, Mrs. T," Rani replied, taking Mrs. Thornsley's hands. "I promise."

Sergeant Dan and his partner, Sergeant Yolanda Osuna, arrived first and began a thorough investigation. "You four kids may help look for clues," Moki's dad said, "but stay away from the pond itself. The water might be toxic. If you find anything, don't touch it. Alert one of us instead. And thanks for calling in Mr. Hobart, Bruce. He's helped our crime lab on some cases," the sergeant said.

"I'm not surprised," Bruce replied as he sat with Mrs. Thornsley to watch the proceedings.

"Well, I guess we can definitely cross off Mr. Hobart as a suspect," Moki said to his friends.

Rani had been scouring the grass around the pond and called out, "Sergeant Dan, look what I found." She pointed downward and smiled for the first time that morning.

It was another business card, a bit waterlogged but current. Rani knew because she had seen one just like it recently. It belonged to Augusta Ramsey.

Sergeant Dan said, "We'll take it to the crime lab to check for fingerprints, but I suspect it's just another plant as Buster Hobart's card was the other day."

"Why do you say that?" Lexi asked. She relished tapping his expertise and wisdom.

"It's too much of a coincidence that we've found two of these on the same premises," he replied. "It's someone's *MO*—method of operation. Sorry for defining that myself, Lanny."

"I smell a frame-up," Lexi said quickly, "and not a very cleverly disguised one at that."

"I'd say you're very perceptive, Lexi," Sergeant Dan replied with a thumbs up.

Sergeant Osuna was inspecting the sphinx's paws and discussing with Lanny whether it was feasible that the rainstorm alone could have done the new damage. "I believe last night's destructive work was done mainly by a person," she said. "Nature only assisted."

"Then I have a theory," Lanny said to everyone. "I believe the prowler returned last night to finish what they had started, taking advantage of the storm's noise and wetness to make us think the earthquake and the rain somehow caused this amount of destruction."

"I think you're on to something, too, Lanny," Sergeant Dan replied, shaking the boy's shoulder.

"Yeah, bro, that makes perfect sense regarding the sphinx," Moki said, "but why was the pond life killed, and how?" At that second, the front doorbell rang.

"I'll bet that's Mr. Hobart now," Mrs. Thornsley said. "I hope he can help answer your questions, Moki."

She excused herself, headed to the front door, and returned a minute later with Buster Hobart. He took one look at the pond he had helped create and sucked in his breath. The detectives noticed that the disgusted look on his face was immediate, suggesting his reactions were genuine. He soon recovered, however, and began to tackle his task. "With your approval, Sergeant Dan, I'm going to bag up some of these dead fish and plants for testing back at my shop."

"Absolutely, Buster," was the officer's instant reply. "You're the expert."

"I'll also take a number of water samples with me, but I can already give you some information just from the odors I'm detecting here. There is a very strong briny smell, which suggests an abnormally high concentration of saline or similar substance present. And given both the plants and fish already exhibit such severe decay, I suspect that a pesticide or herbicide or both were used. I would also like to have Dr. Tessa Kurtz from the zoo test for more specific toxins."

"By all means, call in Dr. Kurtz. Then both of you please send me your reports as soon as possible," Moki's dad replied, thanking the pond shop owner for his help. "For now, let's cover the pond to prevent any other life from being harmed."

Bruce, Buster, and the two police officers hoisted the pond's heavy sectioned night cover over the structure. Last night's storm had prevented Mrs. Thornsley's neighbors from positioning it as they'd been doing for her ever since Dr. Thornsley's death. Everyone thanked Mr. Hobart, who promised speedy results as he left.

Meanwhile Lanny and Rani had been inspecting the sphinx from a distance for clues about its damage. They started whispering excitedly. "Sergeant Dan, may Lanny and I go up onto the pond's stage now and take a closer look at the sphinx?" Rani asked almost breathlessly.

"Yes, but be careful since the sphinx's paws and base extend out over the pond. Avoid touching anything except with a tool," he said.

The two climbed up next to the plaster sphinx and walked around both sides and the back of the statue. They found nothing out of the ordinary, so they returned to what had attracted their attention in the first place.

The others could tell Lanny and Rani were on to

something from the determined looks on their faces. The boy focused his inspection on the paws, then the area of the statue just beyond and below the sphinx's right shoulder. Rani was beaming.

Lanny said, "I'm seeing a hairline crack or break in the plaster in an oval shape by this shoulder." He followed the break line with a tree twig he had picked up nearby. "It looks to me as if someone cut or gouged into the statue, though not too recently, then re-plastered it but didn't do the best job. I never noticed it before, but perhaps the rain—or the prowler—washed away the sandstone coating so the crack is now visible."

Moki's dad stepped onto the stage. "Yes, I agree," he said and took some photographs.

"Sergeant Dan and Mrs. T, may we have permission to chip away at this area to see if our thinking is correct?" It was obvious to the others Lanny was trying hard to remain calm.

"Yes," both adults replied. Mrs. Thornsley found a chisel and hammer in the garden shed and handed them to Rani. She wasted no time in chipping away carefully at the spot by the shoulder. Just as Lanny and Rani thought, the area gave way easily because it was hollow. Light flooded into the cavity from the front where the grooves in the sphinx's paws were cut. Lanny's and Rani's faces lit up in absolute excitement. Sunlight glinted off of something golden that radiated from the opening, immediately capturing the spectators' attention. Everyone stood in silence, almost afraid to breathe. Could it be . . .?

Tucked inside the space, as they suspected, was an Egyptian urn.

# CHAPTER SIXTEEN

· ✧ ·

# Tomb Treasure

"**I**'ll bet you anything we've just found the missing urn," Lanny shouted while gazing into the hollow. Rani nodded her head so excitedly that her long, thick ponytail bobbed up and down.

"Heavens to Betsy!" Mrs. Thornsley almost passed out as Bruce settled her into a patio chair. Here, in all likelihood, was the priceless, stolen urn—and on her property, sealed within a statue that was part of her deceased husband's beloved pond. She was instantly aware that, to others, her husband might look guilty. But never a doubt entered her mind. She knew her husband could never have had anything to do with this atrocity.

Moki and Lexi could not get onto the stage fast enough and, out of carelessness, almost slipped onto the pond cover. Soon, however, they joined their friends in staring down at the treasure.

"This is someone's vicious trick," said Mrs. Thornsley,

recovering enough to stand up. "We must find out who's done this horrible thing to my husband, the pond, and the urn, and why." She looked at the kids, then at the two officers.

"We agree with you one hundred percent, Mrs. T," Moki said, assuming Lanny's role as head detective to prevent the twin boy from contradicting his belief and demanding proof.

The officers, however, had to maintain their objectivity and follow correct police protocol. As tactfully as possible, Sergeant Dan said, "There's more work to do here, everyone. We need conclusive proof as to the guilt of one or more persons, whoever they might be. I'm sure you, of all people, understand that, Lanny. And you should, too, Moki."

Lanny seized his moment. "As a reader of stories starring the logical detective, Sherlock Holmes, and as an amateur detective myself, yes, I do," he replied, eyeing his friends courageously, then jumping down from the pond stage. Moki stared at the ground and bit his lower lip.

"This urn is black with gold lotuses on it and looks like the same size as the one Dr. A described to us," said Rani. "And a cartouche and hieroglyphics—ooh!" Another flash of gold, assisted by the sun, escaped from the concrete cavity.

"I'm calling Dr. Abbott and your parents to come over immediately," Sergeant Dan said to Lanny and Lexi. "We aren't going to run the risk of damaging the urn by trying to remove it ourselves. If the urn is authentic, they'll be overjoyed and very proud of you kids. Then, we'll see what evidence we can gather to resolve this mystery and possibly exonerate Dr. Thornsley." He flashed Mrs. Thornsley a smile and headed to his patrol car.

The kids tried to lessen their impatience for the ARC doctors' arrivals by spending time theorizing, mainly for the adults' sakes, about a chain of events that might explain how the urn came to be hidden on Nutmeg Street. "We're all ears, kids," Bruce said, settling into a high-backed wicker chair next to Mrs. Thornsley.

Lexi began. "We're fairly certain Dr. T was being framed and blackmailed over the urn. It makes sense from the mysterious phone calls he received and the money missing from the bank account. We also think the black-mailer is the one who broke into Dr. T's study looking for something, possibly more money or the picture that went missing. And the blackmailer, the prowler in the study, and Mask Face are the same person."

"What links 'Mask Face,' as you call the trespasser, to the prowler?" Sergeant Osuna asked.

"We believe Mask Face returned to the house and looked in the living room window, hoping no one was home so as to break in again and continue searching in the study," Lexi continued with heads nodding from the squad. "We interfered with that plan by being here."

"That is a logical assumption," the officer said, looking at Sergeant Dan, who had just returned.

"We further believe," added Rani, "that the urn's thief somehow had easy access to the ARC and was there the day the urn arrived, saw Dr. T lock it in his office cabinet, and then returned or sneaked in later that night. The person didn't know the lock's combination, so they cut it off, took the urn, and had to replace the lock, meaning the theft was planned. Remember what Dr. A told us? Dr. T claimed the lock wasn't the same one he had used the night before the theft. Since the new lock looked enough like the old one, the thief could have used the new lock to help others believe Dr. T had stolen the urn and was just pretending not to know the combination. This would have delayed anyone from discovering the urn was missing. The other motive could have been that the real thief wanted to buy a bit more time to hide the urn."

"So, what I think you kids are proposing is if we catch the urn's thief, we'll also be capturing the black-mailer," Sergeant Dan said, pursing his lips and slowly nodding.

"That's right, Dad," Moki replied. "Two for the price of one, so to speak. The thief was smart enough to know it would be easier to get money from Dr. T than to try to peddle a stolen art treasure. The person probably threatened to harm Dr. T, Mrs. T, or the urn—or all three—if Dr. T failed to pay the blackmail and if he refused to accept the blame for the theft."

"It's obvious you're a police officer's son," Sergeant Dan said, slapping Moki on the back.

Lanny crossed his arms over his chest and asked, "Mrs. T, didn't you tell us you and Dr. T were out of town last February, and those odd phone calls started soon after you returned?"

"That's right, Lanyon. Dr. Thornsley had been under such a strain from the theft and the accusations that, once the investigation concluded in January, we left town in early February for a two-week trip to unwind. We returned on Valentine's Day." Mrs. T stared anxiously at the twin.

Lanny said, "Then, my theory is the urn's thief returned to your property while you were away, hid the urn in the sphinx, and patched the spot. The motives were to get the urn out of their possession for the time being, further implicate Dr. T in the theft at some point in the future, begin blackmailing him, and enjoy the irony of the urn being hidden right under Dr. T's nose as part of the pond he loved so much."

Rani snapped her fingers and added, "Recent events—the earthquake and the rainstorm—helped the thief hatch a plan to draw our attention finally to the pond, so we'd find the urn and think Dr. T had put it there himself."

"If all of this is true, kids, we're dealing with one or more cunning criminals who are familiar with the pond and the ARC," Sergeant Dan said with his hands on his hips. "I also have to say, your theories are fascinating and quite probable, but proof is what we need now. I suspect the folks from the ARC will agree. Incidentally, they'll be here soon."

For once, Lanny secretly wished that solid evidence wasn't required.

Sergeant Osuna smiled at the kids and said, "Perhaps Mr. Hobart's and Dr. Kurtz's reports will help, and some other clues will likely develop soon to prove your theories."

At that moment, the doorbell rang. Mrs. Thornsley was exhausted by the day's events, so Bruce went to answer it. He returned with Drs. Abbott, Wyatt, Marlton, and Granger, who almost pranced into the garden out of sheer excitement.

Quick introductions were made. Mrs. Thornsley was given special consideration from everyone, even, if somewhat guardedly, from Dr. Granger. Drs. Wyatt and Marlton hugged and praised all four kids and thanked Bruce and the police officers for being there.

Dr. Abbott could not contain his impatience any longer. "Now, let's take a look at that urn you kids so ingeniously discovered," he said in an uncharacteristically loud voice. Lanny and Rani as the finders had the honor of leading him quickly up onto the pond stage to the sphinx.

Rani pointed and beamed. "Here it is, Dr. Abbott, just as you described it to us."

"From what we could see, it looks just like the urn in Mrs. T's photo," Lexi added.

"Well, ladies and gentlemen, let's see if the object is what we hope it is," said the director, rubbing his hands together and squatting down to begin an examination.

All the eager ARC doctors were up on the stage now,

assisting in the careful removal of the urn. Once it was extricated from its plaster tomb, they found some slight cracks near its base that were deemed repairable. Dr. Granger gazed down into the urn through its cracked seal and observed that the contents appeared to have suffered some damage from the rain.

The kids held their breath waiting for what Dr. Abbott would say. A few moments later, following each doctor's inspection, the urn was declared to be authentic. As if in reply, the treasure gleamed brilliantly in the afternoon sun, seemingly basking in its freedom to enjoy daylight again. The detectives jumped up in a four-way high five.

The ancient artifact was then carefully wrapped and boxed for transport.

# CHAPTER SEVENTEEN

· ✧ ·

# A Clue from Ancient Egypt

"**E**arth to Lexi. Earth to Lexi. Come in, Lexi," Lanny said into his sister's ear the morning after the Egyptian urn was found.

"Huh? . . . uh, what?" she replied dreamily.

"Lexi, you look as if you're far away in another galaxy, certainly not here at the breakfast table. What's up with you?" Lanny took his usual seat next to his sister.

After a brief pause, she looked at her brother intently and said in almost a whisper, "More like back in a distant century. Okay, Lanny, please don't think I'm crazier than you already do, but have you ever sensed spirits at the Thornsleys' house?"

"You mean ancient Egyptian spirits that came from the Valley of the Kings to live on Nutmeg Street? Those kinds of spirits?" Lanny leaned away from his sister, watching her warily.

"Exactly! You believe in them, too, right?" she asked,

making a sudden grab at her brother's arm resting on the kitchen table.

Lanny gazed at his squeezed arm, which Lexi quickly released. Then, he replied, "I admit I've sensed what I imagined to be spirits, especially in Dr. T's study and all around the Egyptian pond. Maybe it's a twin thing—you know, the way we'll walk into a room from opposite parts of the house, humming the same song in the exact same spot at the exact same time. Only now, it's with an idea, though a wonky one."

"Maybe, but I think the spirits followed me home from Mrs. T's yesterday. They kept waking me up last night. I felt they had a message for me, and the message was 'the sphinx has more to tell,'" Lexi replied, her green eyes wide. "For instance, don't you think it's weird that the little sphinx paperweight's right paw was cracked off?"

"Uh, what's so weird about that? We did have an earthquake, you know."

"Lanny, for once, think beyond logic. The paperweight sphinx matches the pond sphinx." She paused, seeing Lanny's confused look. "Don't you get it? The major damage to both was on the right paw, and you and Rani found the urn under the right shoulder."

"The pond-loving twin brother in me says, 'You're right,' but the logical detective in me says, 'You can't be serious.'" He turned away from his sister. "It's a coincidence, that's all. Mmm, I smell bacon." He also spied a bottle of maple syrup on the table.

"Well, anyway, *I* think it's the work of the spirits giving us a clue. We should round up Moki and Rani and go back to Mrs. T's to investigate the sphinx this morning before we go see Mr. Bailey," Lexi said. She reached for Lanny's arm once again to get his attention, but he snatched it away to prevent what he knew all too painfully to be his sister's annoying habit.

Uncle Rocky interrupted, "We're not having our usual Friday-morning poached eggs on whole wheat today." He delivered a plate of food to each twin. "Instead, we're celebrating the return of the urn with—drum roll, please . . ." The twins accommodated him by drumming with their hands on the table edge. "Chocolate chip pancakes, scrambled eggs, and fresh strawberries."

"Smells fabulous as always, Rocky," the twins' dad said, striding toward his place.

"Thanks, Dr. W." Rocky's movements helped waft rich breakfast aromas around the room.

Bruce was long gone to his summer class, but Dr. Marlton joined the group at the table. "We're so proud of you four kids for finding the urn," Mom said, placing her napkin across her lap.

"Yes, we are," Dad added. "Your mother and I felt like the parents of rock stars yesterday afternoon when the word spread around the ARC that the urn had been re-covered. Dr. Abbott smiled so hard all afternoon, I thought his face would crack," Dad joked as he dug into his stack of pancakes.

"Doesn't Sergeant Dan have to hold onto the urn as possible evidence in a crime investigation?" Lanny asked, spooning up some egg bits.

"Yes, but the police chief has given special permission for a team of Egyptologists from the ARC to come to headquarters to begin preparations for the urn's restoration," Mom replied.

"Is there much damage?" Lanny asked as he crunched on some bacon.

"The outside of the urn and the top seal have a few cracks. Some rain water seeped inside and damaged the mummified cobra slightly. Any granular substances that used to be present seem to be gone," Dad replied. He set down his empty orange juice glass.

"Like crystallized cobra venom?" Lexi asked. She popped a strawberry into her mouth.

"Hard to say, my little dreamer," replied Dad, "since the urn was scanned, not emptied. Probably decomposed snake bones and mummification resins and myrrh that were typically applied to the linen wrappings back in ancient times."

"I wonder if any traces ended up in the pond water," Lanny said. "The grooves cut in the sphinx's paws extended into the hollow area where the cracked urn was found."

"I guess we'll just have to wait for the lab test results," Mom replied.

"Those paw grooves are still a mystery, aren't they?" Dad asked.

"Wait. Wait!" Lexi said, standing almost involuntarily. "Lanny's just hit on something important. Maybe something from the urn did drain into the pond. Lanny, sometimes—just sometimes—you're brilliant."

Within the hour, the four kids and Mrs. Thornsley were standing in front of the Egyptian pond. Lexi was given permission to investigate every angle of the damaged sphinx for some clue related to the urn draining into the pond. Within seconds, she beamed and called out, "Wowzers! Guys, come check these out. Not what I was looking for, but . . ."

The other three friends quickly joined her on the pond stage. Lexi was pointing at two small Egyptian hieroglyphics that had been carefully added in black paint to the back of the sphinx's headdress.

Mrs. Thornsley joined the group on the stage. "I remember Dr. Thornsley painting those one afternoon shortly before he passed away. I just thought he was decorating the sphinx."

"I didn't notice those yesterday," Rani said.

"Me neither," Lanny added. "Guess we were too wrapped up in finding the urn. Lexi, are you thinking those hieroglyphics have something to do with the urn draining into the pond?"

Lexi snapped her fingers. "I think it's way beyond that! The hieroglyphs in the cartouche on the left are for King Menes. The ones on the right are for the cobra goddess

Wadjet. But best of all, I think I know why Dr. T painted them, and it wasn't just for decoration. If I'm right, we are about to solve the second part of our mystery, namely, who really stole the urn and why," Lexi shouted. "Follow me, everybody," and she leaped from the stage.

Lexi led the charge into Dr. Thornsley's dark study and started rummaging around in his numerous book-shelves. Mrs. Thornsley flicked on the ceiling light and opened the French doors. Light flooded the room.

*Spirits of ancient Egypt, you brought me this far. Now, please help me one more time*, Lexi begged silently as she scanned title after title. The others stood watching in bewilderment.

"Here it is!" She pulled a thick volume from an eye-level shelf. Emblazoned on the book's cover were the two hieroglyphs identical with those on the stone sphinx. *"King Menes and the Egyptian Goddess Wadjet*, written by Dr. Winston Thornsley," she read from the cover and proudly held up the book.

"Lexi, I know you're about to tell us why this book is so important," Moki said hopefully.

Without a word, Lexi leafed quickly through the timeworn pages. In a few seconds, she stopped, and everyone stared at what she and the book revealed.

"An envelope addressed to you, Mrs. T," she smiled, placing it in the widow's hands. "The hieroglyphics supplied by Dr. T on the sphinx matched those on the book cover. That was a clue Dr. T left for me to help us."

"But how do you think Dr. T knew you'd look on the sphinx's headdress for the clue?" Rani asked.

"Because he knew how much I loved the Egyptian pond and the book he wrote. He must have figured that, eventually, I would find his clue and decipher it!" Lexi replied with a big grin.

"And pretty ironic if Dr. T didn't even know that his clues were right near where the urn was hidden," Lanny added.

"I'd laugh if it wasn't so crummy," Moki said.

Mrs. Thornsley had been staring at the letter and recognized the writing to be her husband's. "Alexia, I think you're right. Dear Dr. Thornsley knew you would understand the clue and find this, especially since you and he used to read his book together in here." The woman's faraway smile mirrored Lexi's.

Mrs. Thornsley's hands began to tremble slightly as she carefully opened the white envelope to reveal a three-page letter and some enclosures. After reading a portion of the letter silently, she sighed deeply, blinked back some tears, and read aloud from the beginning:

*March 31*

*My dearest wife, Ida—*

*If you are finally reading this, it means I have died. I couldn't tell you the truth while I was living because I was too concerned for your safety. Despite my concerns, I have* decided to write this letter because I may soon die. I didn't want the truth to die with me.

I plan to hide this letter well so as to protect you as long as possible from learning about the evil deeds of my younger half-brother, Sebastian Thornsley. You will be in danger if he suspects you know anything about him. You never met him, and I, myself, haven't seen him for over twenty years. Unfortunately, I don't know exactly where he's living now or what name he's using.

I was unaware that Sebastian had apparently come to our town last June after his release from an Indiana state prison. His sole purpose in coming here, he informed me, was to get his revenge by discrediting me due to his long-standing jealously of my fame, fortune, and success.

Sebastian's communications have all been by phone, the first call coming last month shortly after we returned from our February vacation. He demanded $50,000 from me as ransom for the safe return of the Egyptian urn, <u>which he admitted stealing</u> from my office last October.

He further stipulated that I must keep his identity and guilt a secret and take the blame myself. In other words, I was framed and made the patsy for his crimes. He said if I failed to follow his instructions, he would destroy the urn and harm you.

To prove that Sebastian was, in fact, my relative, he sent me an exact duplicate of the old family photograph I had on my study desk. I have enclosed both copies, his and mine, in this letter and apologize for not being truthful with you when I told you the photo's frame had been broken. Actually, I had hidden the photo from you. Again, it was to protect you from possibly discovering who Sebastian was and then being injured by him before you found this letter. He is the person on the far left in the group shot. Hopefully, Sebastian can be identified and caught.

The $50,000 ransom is due tomorrow, April 1, and I intend to pay it. I doubt that my half-brother will keep his part of the bargain and return the urn undamaged and leave us alone. But if the blackmail payment keeps you safe, even for a short time, then it is worth every penny.

Before doing anything else, please show this letter to Dr. Abbott and ask him to help you obtain immediate police protection.

My sincere hope is that the urn will be returned safely to me tomorrow, that Sebastian will be caught and brought to justice for his crimes, and that we will suffer no further harm from him.

As for myself, this entire ordeal—from the urn's theft last

*fall, the inquest, and the smearing of my name and reputation, to the blackmailing and deception now—has taxed every fiber of my body, mind, and spirit. I strongly doubt I will live to see Sebastian answer for what he's done.*

*Ida, my loving wife, thank you for your enduring love and support all these fifty years but especially in these last few months since the urn's theft. I know that you have always believed in me. Be safe, well, and happy.*

*All my love for eternity,*

*Your husband, Winston*

"I always knew my husband was innocent and something sinister was happening to him," Mrs. Thornsley said after finishing the letter. "He took the blame to protect me and planned to continue protecting me, even after he died." She dissolved in tears, the letter and photos falling from her hands.

The boys shuffled their feet, not sure what else to do. Both Rani and Lexi, however, joined Mrs. Thornsley, hands clasped, in a bout of crying. Their tears were a strange mix. Some were for joy at knowing how much Dr. T loved his wife and that they now had the means to capture the real thief. But there were many tears of sorrow for all Dr. and Mrs. Thornsley had endured at the hands of the scheming, sadistic Sebastian Thornsley.

After a few moments, Lanny ventured to say, "The good news, Mrs. T, is the letter exonerates Dr. T from the urn's theft and gives us the motive and possible identity of the real thief."

No one else commented immediately. The shock delivered by the letter had seemingly sucked every molecule of oxygen right out of the room. It took some time before the breeze drifting in through the study doors replenished the supply.

Shortly, Lexi succeeded at taking some deep breaths, threw back her shoulders, and brushed the tears off her face. Then, she picked up the letter and enclosures from the rug and judiciously began examining the small man in both photographs, occasionally fighting back some lingering sobs.

Moki rallied himself to hug Mrs. Thornsley while Lanny offered Rani a tissue.

Before long, Lexi had another astonishing announcement. The others gathered around her. "Check this out. I'm looking at the person Dr. T identified as Sebastian Thornsley, the man guilty of these crimes. And, I'll bet, the same man who damaged the sphinx and poisoned the pond. Unless I'm greatly mistaken, we are about to solve our case. I know who he is and where we can find him."

# CHAPTER EIGHTEEN

· ✧ ·

# Help from Modern Science

Mrs. Thornsley wiped away her tears as she recovered from reading the letter. She allowed Moki to lead her across the room to join Lanny and Rani, who were looking over Lexi's shoulder at the man in the photographs.

"The man Dr. T identified as Sebastian Thornsley was right here on Nutmeg Street just last Monday," Lexi announced. She jabbed repeatedly at the photo. "Yeah, I'm sure of it now! The eyes and mouth give him away. He is none other than Mr. Sam Bailey, the mason from Seeds Sow Fine Gardeners." Her lips were pinched as she gazed at his image.

"But Alexia, how can that be?" asked Mrs. Thornsley. "Sam Bailey worked with Dr. Thornsley on the planning and building of the pond last summer. The man was here almost daily. Surely my husband would have recognized him then." She sighed, and her hand fell limply away from the photograph's edge.

"Mrs. T, did Dr. T have many face-to-face talks with Mr. Bailey about the Egyptian pond?" Lanny asked. He remembered Buster Hobart's description of the shy mason.

"Well, Lanyon, now that you mention it, my husband did most of his dealings with Mr. Hobart. Sam Bailey stayed in the background and wore sunglasses and a big hat," the widow replied. Her hand rose quickly to grip the photograph's edge once again.

Lexi said, "I think Mr. Bailey's disguise and the fact that a person's appearance can change a lot over twenty years, especially someone who's been in prison as Mr. Bailey was, could cause Dr. T not to recognize his own brother. When we saw Mr. Bailey in your garden the other day, he wasn't in disguise. No hat. No sunglasses. Remember?"

Rani snapped her fingers. "Some of our theories were correct, then. We now know the identity of the thief and blackmailer. And now, I definitely believe Sebastian Thornsley, aka Sam Bailey, broke into this study recently to search for these pictures. He probably intended to take them back all along but couldn't due to Dr. T's death. He probably didn't want to run the risk of being identified from them as Lexi has just done."

"Then 'small' Sebastian Thornsley, aka 'agile' Sam Bailey is also the small and agile Mask Face," Moki said. "Whoa! Now I remember how he jumped onto the pond stage like a cat when he saw Tortuga."

"And Parking Lot Man, who tried to run us down at the beach. Same sedan," Lexi grinned.

"But we also need evidence about the parts, if any, played by our other Persons of Interest," Rani said, twisting the ends of her long ponytail. "Right, Lanny?"

"It's just a matter of time now," Lanny replied, smiling at her confidently.

"Let's check with Dr. A to see if Sam Bailey could have been at the ARC the day the urn arrived," Moki said. "If Sam *had* worked indoors, he might have secretly followed Dr. T to his office to see where the urn would be stored. He might have noticed the cabinet's lock brand and type, eventually making the theft and frame-up that much easier for him to pull off."

"And bro," Lanny said, "you were correct when you hypothesized recently about the blackmailer wanting money more than the urn, probably realizing that trying to sell the urn internationally would result in his getting arrested, pronto." He gently punched Moki's arm.

"I think it's time for us to call Sergeant Dan, Dr. A, Uncle Rocky, and Bruce to give them the good news that we have cracked this case wide open," Lexi said. "Mrs. T, would you like to come with us to the ARC and bring the letter and photos yourself?"

"Oh boy, would I," the widow replied, almost dancing. "I've hoped this day would come, and it has, thanks to you four wonderful detectives."

Sergeant Dan and Bruce arrived on Nutmeg Street almost

simultaneously and were amazed as the kids and Mrs. Thornsley brought them up to date on the evidence from the letter and its enclosures.

The group caravanned to the ARC. Sergeant Dan called Buster Hobart and Tessa Kurtz en route and asked them to meet the large party in Dr. Abbott's office with their findings regarding the toxic pond. Drs. Abbott, Wyatt, Marlton, and Granger were eagerly awaiting everyone's arrival.

Each guest was ushered into Dr. Abbott's office. A shaken Mrs. Thornsley asked Alexia to read the letter aloud while she sipped some of the director's hot tea. The group listened, spellbound.

After the reading, the four kids clarified for the adults how and why Dr. Thornsley had been framed for the crime. They shared the photographs as proof that Sebastian Thornsley and Sam Bailey were one and the same person who had committed the crimes, including the likelihood that he was also the sedan-driving Mask Face. Everyone was overjoyed, hugging the kids or patting them on the back. The detectives had worked hard, and Dr. Thornsley could finally be exonerated of the theft. In addition, the identity of the real criminal was nearly certain.

Sergeant Dan still wanted to verify Sam Bailey's identity. He left the room briefly to get Ms. Graham's help in faxing one of the photos to the Indiana prison warden.

"Dr. Abbott, is it possible Mr. Bailey could have been here at the ARC the day the urn arrived?" Moki asked. He sat forward in his chair at Dr. Abbott's large conference table.

"It's more than possible, Moki. It's a fact. Before your arrival, Ms. Graham and I looked back at last October's calendar and discovered the gardening company was indeed at the ARC then. I have personally called the owner who confirmed Sam Bailey had been among the masons and gardeners who had been sent here that very day."

Moki said, "We figured if Mr. Bailey was inside the ARC the day the urn arrived, he might have followed Dr. T up to his office and observed where the urn was stored. Then he probably hid somewhere inside the building or returned later that day and stole it."

Lanny added, "We also believe Mr. Bailey changed the lock to implicate Dr. T further as a thief who wanted to delay, for his own sake, anyone from finding out the urn was missing."

"We'll confront him with your suppositions after he's arrested," Sergeant Dan cut in, having returned with the information from Indiana. "Here is what I have just learned about Sebastian Thornsley, who is indeed Sam Bailey. He is also known as Snitch Bailey among his former inmates. He was released from prison last June and indicated he was heading to California 'to begin his life anew and to be reunited with his long-time girlfriend and his dear older half-brother.'"

"Oh, bruddah!" Moki whispered to Lanny, who shook his head in disbelief.

"'Girlfriend'?—hmm . . . Augusta Ramsey, no doubt,"

Rani said, slapping her clinched fist into the palm of her other hand. "Now, we have the link."

"Just curious, Mrs. T, but did anyone in Dr. T's family have the last name Bailey?" Lexi asked.

"Why, yes, Alexia. It was the maiden name of my late husband's paternal grandmother, which makes sense that Sam Bailey would select it since he and my late husband apparently had the same father."

"Rani thinks she's figured out Sam Bailey's— Snitch's—plan regarding the hiding of the urn at the Egyptian pond," Lanny said to everyone. All eyes focused on her.

Rani said, "Snitch must have learned somehow that Dr. and Mrs. T were going out of town in February. Then he sneaked onto their property in the night, hid the urn in the sphinx, and patched the spot. His motives were to get the urn out of his possession for the time being and to further implicate Dr. T in the theft somehow in the future. He also planned to begin blackmailing Dr. T and to enjoy the fact that the urn was hidden right under Dr. T's nose as part of the pond he loved so much. Obviously, he never intended to return the artifact, even after the blackmail was paid."

Lanny jabbed at the tabletop and said, "I want to hear Snitch admit he planned for us to find the urn by using the earthquake, the rainstorm, and the pond poisoning to draw our attention to the spot. He obviously wanted to make all of us think a guilty Dr. T had hidden it there himself."

"And I hope to hear him admit to being the blue car owner, Mask Face," Moki added.

"Lanny, specifically, how did Sam Bailey, or Sam Thornsley, or Snitch—whatever he calls himself—use the pond this past week to lead you to the urn?" Dr. Granger asked softly.

The boy replied, "We saw Mr. Bailey inspect the pond statues when he was at Mrs. T's. He must have noticed then there were grooves in the sphinx's paws from the earthquake. Being a mason and a gardener, he probably also knew rain was forecast for midweek. We believe he decided to use the grooves and the rain to hatch his plan. That if he made the grooves deeper—which he did that night when Mrs. T heard him tapping by the pond—the rainwater would eventually flood into the hollow chamber where he had previously hidden the urn. He had purposely damaged it to make us believe the pond's poison came from the venom of the urn's mummified cobra, as Lexi suspected. To implicate Dr. T, he returned a second night during the storm and poisoned the pond, hoping it would lead to a thorough investigation and, most likely, the discovery of the urn, which it did."

"Dr. Kurtz and I can add to that theory from what we found in the pond water," Buster Hobart added, thumbing through his written report. "Apparently, Sam Bailey wanted all of us to believe something toxic from the urn drained into the pond, and once the substances were identified, it would point to the urn being nearby."

Lexi added, "Lanny, you said as much at breakfast this morning when you wondered if anything from the urn might have drained into the pond from the grooves that extended into the hollow chamber." She couldn't help but eye her brother proudly. "Plus, the sphinx's paws extend out over the pond, making it entirely possible for something to have leaked into the water. I was hoping to find evidence of that this morning but got distracted by the hieroglyphics on the sphinx."

"And I for one am so thankful that you did get distracted," Mrs. Thornsley said.

"This is all very interesting," said Sergeant Dan as he entered notes into his mobile device. "Dr. Kurtz and Mr. Hobart, what were the lab test results from the pond water and animal specimens?"

Buster Hobart began. "I found high concentrations of sodium chlorate, a nonselective herbicide available at some garden shops and toxic to all green plant parts. I also found a lot of soda ash, more specifically, a type of natron, which could have killed the fish and plants."

The four kids' eyes lit up. "Sam Bailey's lunch receipt that Tortuga found by the pond places him near a natron pit in Desert County," Lanny added, catching his parents' proud smiles.

"Could it be natron from the urn when the cobra was mummified instead?" Lexi wondered, still hoping for an ancient Egyptian connection.

"Highly unlikely," Buster said, "since there was too

much of the substance in the pond, and it was mostly hydrated soda ash and minerals, different from ancient natron. Once again, I think the crafty Sam Bailey *wanted* us to conclude it was from ancient times, therefore from the urn, but it wasn't. He made a mistake by using too much of the wrong ingredient, and he probably did get the soda ash out in Desert County, the most likely source."

"Speaking of mistakes, Mr. Bailey made more," said Dr. Kurtz, holding up her report folder. "I found an extremely dense and deadly concentration of cobratoxin—but not from an Egyptian cobra. The substance was hannahtoxin, the kind present in king cobra venom. King cobras live in India and throughout Southeast Asia, not Egypt," she smirked. "In short, Mr. Bailey didn't research cobras very thoroughly, if at all."

Rani snapped her fingers. "Wait a minute! Could that explain the recent disappearance of cobra venom from the Cactusville Reptile Gardens?"

"Yes, it could," the herpetologist replied. "Given that five vials of king cobra venom were stolen, I think we can conclude all of them ended up in the Thornsley pond. It didn't kill the plants and fish since it had to be injected to be harmful, unless the fish had wounds that would allow the venom's entry. I think we can say the venom, like the other toxins, was added merely to point you to the urn."

"Then that would seem to implicate Augusta Ramsey since we saw her at the gift shop from the reptile gardens where the venom had already been stolen," Moki said.

"I'm thinking she knew her way around the grounds, more than just the gift shop." The boy was sitting at attention.

"Are you saying the criminal returned to the scene of the crime?" Lanny asked.

"In this case, close enough to the scene," Moki replied with a thumbs up.

"We police refer to that kind of action as 'returning to refute guilt,'" Sergeant Dan said.

"Pretty foolish—or clever—of her, depending upon how daring she was," Lexi added. "Or maybe she went back out of curiosity to see if her crime had been noticed by anyone there."

"Well, one thing's for sure," Rani said. "Either Ms. Ramsey didn't do her snake research, or she just didn't read the labels on the refrigerated vials of venom and stole the wrong kind."

"Yes, and all of that might mean Snitch Bailey is also one or more of our other mysterious Persons of Interest," Lexi replied. "Maybe he pushed Moki into the pit and later received the two packages, possibly the venom, from Ms. Ramsey in front of her shop. He was probably also in her back office and helped her push the plaster cobra over onto Lanny and me. Afterwards, he spied on us from the alley. And later, he tried to run us down at the beach. He wanted us out of the way, permanently."

"Whoa, wait a minute," Lanny said. "Why would Ms. Ramsey take such a big risk by being Snitch's accomplice? Just because she might be his girlfriend? What did she stand to gain? It would have to be something of great value. All of this needs to be investigated," the boy said as the squad's enthusiasm jerked to a halt. The three detectives knew Lanny, the stickler for evidence, was correct.

"Now that's thinking like Sherlock Holmes," Sergeant Dan replied, nodding at Lanny. "I agree, kids. Her connection to Snitch, the girlfriend angle, and her motives need looking into."

"Well, Sergeant Dan, kids, and everyone, thank you for a job very well done so far," Dr. Abbott said. He stood and shook each guest's hand across the table. "This is all, indeed, quite remarkable. I think we can conclude that the urn's theft, its later concealment in the pond's sphinx, and the pond poisoning had to have been done by someone very much alive now—like Sam 'Snitch' Bailey. Mrs. Thornsley, I intend to exonerate your husband formally once and for all, locally and worldwide," Dr. Abbott said. He looked to Sergeant Dan, who nodded his approval.

Mrs. Thornsley cried tears of joy and was surrounded by the girls first, then by the boys. Lexi and Rani doled out hugs all around while Lanny and Moki high-fived everyone, including Mrs. Thornsley. The noise brought Ms. Graham running into her boss's office where she quickly joined in the celebration.

After the cheering died down, Sergeant Dan said, "I now have enough evidence to issue a warrant for Sam 'Snitch' Bailey's arrest within the hour."

Moki cracked a cagey smile. "With all due respect, Dad, is it possible to hold off arresting him for a while? I have a plan that could help us capture both Snitch Bailey and his accomplice, most likely Augusta Ramsey, tonight."

# CHAPTER NINETEEN

· ✧ ·

# Snitch

"What's your plan, son?" the sergeant asked Moki as the ARC meeting was ending.

"First, no word has leaked to the media yet that the urn has been recovered, has it?" Moki asked Dr. Abbott and Ms. Graham.

"That's right, Moki," Dr. Abbott replied. "Your dad asked us to keep the information within the building yesterday after you four found the urn, and that was the order I gave."

"Good," Moki said with a glint in his eye. "Then Snitch and his accomplice have to be wondering right about now why they haven't heard anything in the news yet about the urn's miraculous recovery on Mrs. T's property and about the Egyptologist's 'obvious' guilt."

"That's brilliant, Moki," Dr. Marlton said with a big grin. "So, you think by continuing to keep the found treasure a secret, it will force Snitch and his accomplice out into the open to investigate out of sheer anxiety?"

"That's exactly what I'm thinking," he replied. "I also think the Botanic Hill Detectives should wait by the Egyptian pond tonight. I don't think it will take long after dark for Snitch and company to show up to see if the urn has been found." Moki looked at each of them.

Everyone present, including Buster Hobart, Dr. Kurtz, and Dr. Abbott, agreed that Moki did, indeed, have a clever ambush plan. Bruce knew this repeated the strategy the kids had already used during their "sleepover" at Mrs. Thornsley's but said nothing. Lanny caught the tutor's eye and silently thanked him for not ratting on them.

Sergeant Dan said, "All right, but I can't condone you four doing that alone." The twins' parents quickly voiced their agreement with the officer. Sergeant Dan continued, "Two of us will stand watch in the garden with you tonight. Moki, how about you and Lexi being with me? Then Lanny, Rani, and perhaps Bruce can be in the other group." Bruce was more than willing to participate, and everyone nodded their approval of the plan.

Rani excused herself and called home. Upon returning to the group, she said with dancing eyes, "My parents are thrilled and proud we have solved our case and are fine with tonight's plan as long as Sergeant Dan and Bruce are with us at Mrs. T's." Lexi beamed and hugged her friend.

After finalizing more plans and discussing pre-cautions, the group broke up to prepare for the exciting night ahead. The four kids were mildly disgruntled, however, that two adults would be participating in what they had hoped would be their big chance to finally crack the case all by themselves.

The six ambushers quietly slipped through Mrs. Thornsley's back door by eight p.m. and discussed their hiding places.

Moki was fidgety. "I want this plan to work, especially since I came up with it. Mrs. T, do you have any more of those chocolate chip cookies? They might help calm my nerves," he said as he looked toward the dining room table.

"How can more sugar calm you?" Lexi asked, making a face.

Before he could answer, the woman handed him an extra-large cookie from a nearby plate, and the boy downed it in under a minute. Everyone moved into the living room. Then, as planned, Mrs. Thornsley turned out the last light on the first floor, pitching the entire house into darkness. She clicked on a flashlight. Its narrow yellow beam danced upon the stairs and wall as it showed her the way to her bedroom on the second floor.

After seeing that Mrs. Thornsley was safely upstairs, the four detectives, Bruce, and Sergeant Dan tiptoed out into the side yard and concealed themselves among the pond's foliage and the garden's bushes. Moki licked cookie crumbs from his lips and prepared for the wait, convinced he was calmer now.

An hour dragged by, which seemed like an ancient Egyptian eternity to all the watchers. Lexi decided not to pretend she was an Egyptologist this time in order to stay alert. She couldn't help notice the poor pond, however, which was still covered. Buster Hobart had promised to start cleaning it once he got the go-ahead from Sergeant Dan. It couldn't be soon enough. Lexi decided she would buy Mrs. Thornsley another new lotus to celebrate when the pond was finally restored.

The moonless night made observation difficult, so the watchers had to rely mainly on their ears. Their diligence paid off when, shortly after ten, a rustling sound was heard. Someone was creeping across the side yard lawn. Something crackled near the low-hanging tree branches. The six ambushers were instantly on alert as they spied a dark shape approaching.

An intruder of small build, dressed in dark clothing, slinked toward the pond. With a flashlight on low, the snoop must have finally noticed the pond was covered and in ruins as evidenced by the long pause that enabled the beam to play reassuringly over the area. The six ambushers held their breath and their places.

Like a cat, the wiry intruder noiselessly and effortlessly jumped onto the pond stage, apparently to inspect the sphinx and see if the urn had been found. Sure enough, the flashlight beam was trained on the right side of the sphinx, the very spot Rani and Lanny had hollowed out.

The intruder froze. The urn had been discovered after

all. But why hadn't the valuable find been on the news? That could mean only one thing. A trap! The intruder turned, obviously hoping to get out of the yard before being captured.

But it was too late. The four kids followed by Sergeant Dan and Bruce emerged from their hiding places and pounced upon the startled criminal, shining their own flashlights at full power into the angry man's face.

"It's all over, Snitch. Give up quietly," Sergeant Dan said with his hand resting on top of his holster. He easily clinched the man's small wrists, then pulled the tight black hood from his head before clapping Snitch Bailey into handcuffs.

"You kids, you think you're so smart," Snitch sputtered and glared at the four.

"Correction, Snitch," replied Bruce. "They don't just think they're smart—they *are* smart. In fact, *brilliant* is a better word." He smirked at the man writhing within the officer's grip.

Sergeant Dan continued, "To begin, you're under arrest for the theft of the urn, destruction of private property, the blackmail of Dr. Thornsley, and the attempted murder of the four kids present. I'm certain we'll add many more charges tomorrow. Now, I'll read you your rights. You have the right to remain silent when questioned. Anything you say can—" but the officer was abruptly cut off.

"You and I both know I've heard it before," snapped

Snitch, squirming to look at the sergeant. "I know I'm done for, what with my prison record."

At that moment, two people entered the yard from the side gate. All heads turned. "Look who I caught getting out of a blue sedan's driver seat and sneaking into the garden," said Sergeant Osuna. Sergeant Dan's partner had been staking out the Nutmeg Street property from around the corner. Firmly in the officer's grip squirmed Snitch's accomplice, Augusta Ramsey herself.

"I told you to stay put in the car," Snitch barked at her with a scowl.

"When you didn't come back, I got worried. You know I care about you, so I came to find you and make sure you were all right." There was a decided catch in her voice.

"Care about me? Find me? Well, I don't care about you. You've never been my girlfriend, despite what you seem to think. Business partner, maybe, but even that's a stretch." Snitch's eyes looked like shooting sparks as he jerked away from Augusta.

"Looks as if you've both been 'found,'" Lanny said. He and Moki high-fived one another.

Sergeant Dan repeated the Miranda warning to the accomplice and warned Snitch again to remain silent for the time being.

"I'm not talking until I have an attorney," Augusta Ramsey said, growling at all present, but then added, "You better not put the finger on me, Snitch! This was all your idea. I thought I might end up with this pair of silver bracelets, but I did it because I cared about you. And I trusted you!" shouted the woman as she was handcuffed. "Fine thanks I get."

"Augusta, you should know Snitch left your business card here by the pond the other day. Looks as if he tried to make you another one of his patsies in this horrific caper," Sergeant Dan said.

"Why you—!" Augusta said, her red face and blazing eyes trained on Snitch. She tried to lunge at him, but Sergeant Osuna held her captive fast.

Thanks to the Hobart and Kurtz reports, Lexi and Lanny outlined all the mistakes the pair had made in their toxic pond brew. The criminals' contempt for one another's botching of the plan grew along with their kicking and shouting.

"Dunce!" Snitch shouted, glaring fire at his partner in crime.

"Me? You were the small brains—I repeat, *small*—behind this scheme," Augusta replied. "And to think I believed you and trusted you when you promised to share half of the blackmail money with me. Guess that does make me a dunce after all."

Augusta and Snitch were taken into custody by Sergeant Osuna as they kicked, hurled blame, and snapped more insults at one another. A back-up police car had arrived, and each suspect was soon whisked off to police head-quarters separately. Mrs. Thornsley had somehow slept through all of it.

"I guess we could say Snitch snitched on her," Moki said, watching the police cars roar off down Nutmeg Street. Once they were out of sight, he turned and high-fived Lanny again.

"Yeah, and she snitched on him," Rani replied, high-fiving Lexi. "Come on. Let's go tell Mrs. T the good news, then go over to my house. I'll make us all a big bowl of mac 'n' cheese."

# CHAPTER TWENTY

· ✧ ·

# Festival and Celebrations

The townspeople had much to celebrate at the opening of the Las Palmitas Paradise Days Festival in late August. Dr. Abbott had been true to his word, seeing to it that Dr. Thornsley's fine reputation was reinstated worldwide. In addition, he posthumously presented the Egyptologist with the ARC's Most Honored Scientist Award during the festival. Even Dr. Granger supported the idea.

The police investigation and the trials of Snitch Bailey and Augusta Ramsey had been completed. The criminals' confessions and the evidence presented against them corroborated all the Botanic Hill detectives' theories. The pair were convicted of each crime for which they had been accused and sentenced to many years in prison.

Snitch Bailey had admitted to being all the Persons of Interest, wearing disguises to pull off his sinister caper and to attempt to harm or intimidate the kids away from his trail.

He also revealed that he had hidden inside the ARC near the Egyptologist's office before stealing the urn and had spied on the Thornsleys from their garden, overhearing their February travel plans.

Augusta Ramsey had explained that one package she had given Snitch outside her shop contained the five vials of cobra venom, which she had, indeed, stolen from Cactusville. The second box contained the natron Snitch had stolen from Desert County. She had taken the substance after Snitch first stole it, not trusting him to conceal it properly.

Snitch also revealed during the trial that two events had seemed beyond good luck. First, the Egyptologist had called the garden shop the year before to hire a mason to design and build a pond. Bailey had learned his craft in prison and was perfect for the job. Then, the Egyptian urn arrived at the ARC. The opportunity to gain access to his half-brother, steal the urn, and get revenge on the scientist, literally, in his own backyard, was too much for the two criminals to pass up.

Fortunately, the Egyptian urn had been repaired in time for the festival. It was on public display at the ARC. In addition, every dollar of the blackmail money had been found in an old suitcase in the back office at Ancient Sands Curio Shop and returned to Mrs. Thornsley.

On September first, some guests, including everyone who

had been present in Dr. Abbott's office that late June day when the kids had cracked the case, assembled by the Egyptian pond on Nutmeg Street. Mrs. Thornsley had organized a special party. Today would have been Dr. Thornsley's seventy-fifth birthday, and the widow wanted to remember him fondly and happily, surrounded by all her friends, new and old.

Some party-goers were gazing hungrily at the large chocolate sheet cake Uncle Rocky had made for the occasion. He had even remembered the candles, thanks to Lexi. Others were admiring Buster Hobart's quality restoration of the pond. It was back to its original splendor. Lexi's gift of a pink lotus floated lazily upon the shimmering surface. Moki had bought a few goldfish for the pond, even though he thought they looked like silly, colorful guppies compared to giant koi. The statues of Anubis and Horus had also been repaired, but work hadn't started yet on the pitiful sphinx.

Moki was entertaining the group by leading everyone in the song, *Hau'oli Lā Hānau*, or "Happy Birthday," in Hawaiian. Mrs. Thornsley was all smiles. "Moki, you're a dream," she said.

"I think so, too," Lexi admitted, winking at the boy. The girl had just returned to the garden terrace from Dr. Thornsley's study where she had reshelved his book on Menes and Wadjet. Mrs. Thornsley had encouraged her to share it with the guests, showing them the exact page where Lexi had found the important letter that finally broke the case wide open.

Now in Lexi's hand was the formerly damaged sand-stone sphinx paperweight from Dr. Thornsley's desk. The paw was so well repaired that not even a hairline crack was visible. "Mrs. T, you did a great job fixing the little sphinx," Lexi said, first holding it out for others to inspect.

"It gave me a good reason to go back into the study, which wasn't easy, as you know, after my husband's death," she replied. She carefully took the figurine and cradled it in her hands.

"Speaking of sphinxes," Dr. Abbott said in a loud voice, "we have a special presentation for you, Mrs. Thornsley, to commemorate further your late husband."

He nodded in the direction of the garden gate. All eyes turned to see Dr. Granger, Dr. and Mrs. Kumar, Dr. Kurtz, Sergeant Dan, Buster Hobart, and the twins' parents carrying something heavy toward them. Mrs. Thornsley removed its burlap cover. It was an exact duplicate of the pond's sphinx, but without the damage Snitch had inflicted upon the original.

"Oh, it's so beautiful!" Mrs. Thornsley said as she rubbed her hand lovingly over the statue's sandstone surface. "Thank you all for this. The pond is now complete. I know my husband would be pleased. I will think of all of you and the happy conclusion of the mystery every time I look at it."

"We've arranged for a newly hired mason to come Monday from Seeds Sow Fine Gardeners to install it for you," Dr. Abbott said, looking up to catch many stares.

"Now, don't worry—Sergeant Dan's already run a check on him, and he's all right within the law." Everyone chuckled.

"Well, the presentations aren't over yet," the widow announced. "I would like to give each of my four special detectives a keepsake to thank them for all their hard work on this case."

She handed each detective a gold-plated reclining sphinx, the same size as the repaired paperweight. The black onyx eyes shone enigmatically. The kids' names were engraved on the bottom of each with the year and the inscription, "Thanks for solving the Nutmeg Street mystery. Love, Dr. and Mrs. T."

Rani held hers up and asked it, "So, what secrets are you keeping?"

Mrs. Thornsley replied, "Well, if it is keeping any secrets, I'm sure you kids will find out."

"Now, it's our turn to make a presentation," Lanny added, following the guests' applause.

The kids called the ARC's director forward. Lanny said, "Dr. Abbott, we four have decided to give you and the ARC the reward money we received from the police department for solving the case. We are wondering if you could use it to set up a memorial scholarship in Dr. T's name for a deserving Egyptology student." Each handed him their check.

"Why, yes. I'm honored and overwhelmed but not surprised," the director replied while staring at the items thrust into his hands. "You four are certainly generous. The ARC thanks you."

At that very second, the guests felt some mild shaking underfoot. "Oh, no. Not another earthquake," Uncle Rocky said, shaking his sphinxlike head. "Here we go again. Isn't this how it all started a few months ago?"

"Just a little tremor. Nothing to worry about," Rani's geologist dad explained with a wink.

The rest of the pleasant, warm afternoon was spent devouring every crumb of the delectable birthday cake and enjoying more stories about Dr. Thornsley's many excavations and adventures in Egypt.

Toward the end of the day, despite the merriment, the four kids began to notice a tinge of sadness slowly gaining a hold of them. Their case was over. Would another mystery come their way soon and bring the adventures they craved?

Dr. Wyatt noticed their sullen moods. "Twins, your Aunt Connie Marlton is arriving next weekend from Washington, D.C. She's photographing the ARC's *Gemstones of Antiquity* exhibit."

"Super!" Lexi said, her eyes and smile widening. Aunt Connie, a renowned photojournalist and Dr. Marlton's younger sister, was one of her favorite relatives. "She'll be fun to have around, especially now that there's no mystery. You know, though, gemstones can be mysterious. Hmm."

All four kids did their best to stay cheerful so as not to spoil the party. If they had only suspected adventure would soon be abundantly theirs again, they would have been heartened to know their next daring mystery was already simmering not too far away on Eucalyptus Street.

✧   ✧   ✧

Kids—Thank you for buying and reading my book! If you enjoyed it, I would love for you to _leave a review online_. Feel free to contact me, too.

You can also sign up for my _monthly newsletter_, geared to kids, in order to follow the Botanic Hill detectives at **www.sherrilljoseph.com/newsletter**.

And if you want to rejoin the Botanic Hill detectives for their next adventure in the series, please watch for **Eucalyptus Street: Green Curse** _coming soon_. You will be challenged by a mysterious old mansion, a seventy-year-old puzzle poem, dusty secret passages, a hidden gemstone, and a flickering light in the nearby cemetery. Until then, thanks, and keep reading and writing!

↳ _Now available!_ ♡ S.J.

# MOKI AND ALOHA'S HAWAIIAN DICTIONARY

*The following important information about the Hawaiian alphabet and language was adapted from the helpful Website, www.alohafriends.com.*

## The Hawaiian Alphabet and Language

The entire Hawaiian alphabet is made up of the five vowels: **a, e, i, o, u**, and only seven consonants: **h, k, l, m, n, p, and w.**

In the Hawaiian language, a consonant is always followed by a vowel. All Hawaiian words, therefore, end in a vowel, never in a consonant.

To help pronounce Hawaiian words, break them down into single-syllable chunks, often with just two letters per syllable. Sometimes the letter *W* is pronounced the same as *V* as in the traditional pronunciation of *Hawai'i,* which is phonetically pronounced *huh-VI-ee* rather than *huh-WI-ee*; and, for *Haleiwa,* which is phonetically pronounced *hah-lay-EE-vuh* rather than *hah-lay-EE-wuh.*

A punctuation mark called an *'okina,* which looks like a backward English-language apostrophe, is a glottal stop, meaning that each vowel is pronounced; for example, o'o = *oh-oh.*

Another mark is the *kahakō*, a macron, which looks like a line over a vowel. It signals that the vowel should be held longer and stressed; for example, in the word *kahakō*, the o sound would be held longer and stressed when pronounced. And be warned: Leaving out the *kahakō* can change the meaning of a word; for example, *kāne* means male, but *kane* means skin disease.

## Hawaiian Vowel Sounds Pronunciation Key

| | |
|---|---|
| E = **ay** as long a in *bay* | A = **uh** as in *about* |
| I = **ee** as long e in *bee* | A = **ah** as in *all* |
| AI = **i** as long i in *ice* | AU = **ow** as in *ouch* |
| O = **o** as long o in *ocean* | E = **eh** as in *effort* |
| U = **oo** as long u in *new* | OI = **oi** as in *boy* |
| EI = **ay** as long a in *bay* | |

# Hawaiian Words and Definitions from Our Story
*Stress the capitalized syllables.*
*Use the pronunciation key on the previous page to help.*

**akamai**— adj. *AH-kah-mi*; smart

**aloha**— interj. *uh-LO-hah*; hello; good-bye; I love you

**Hauʻoli Lā Hānau**— interj. *how-O-lee-lah-hah-now*; Happy Birthday

**honu**— n. *HO-noo*; sea turtle

**kalani/Kalani**— n. *kuh-LAH-nee*; the sky; Moki, Aloha, and Sergeant Dan's last name

**kāne**— n. *KAH-nay*; male; man; men

**keiki**— n. *KAY-kee*; child; children; kid; kids

**kuʻuipo**— n. *koo-oo-EE-po*; sweetheart

**mahalo**— interj. *muh-HAH-lo*; thank you; thanks

**mahalo nui loa**— interj. *muh-HAH-lo-noo-ee-LO-uh*; thank you very much

**(_____) no ka oi**— v./adj. *no-kah-OI*; (fill in the blank) is the best, for example, Hawaiʻi no ka oi, meaning Hawaiʻi is the best

**Oʻahu**— n. *o-AH-whoo*; third largest of the eight main Hawaiian islands; home of the state's capital, Honolulu; Moki's birthplace

**ohana**— n. *o-HAH-nuh*; family

**pau/all pau**— adj. *POW/ahl-POW*; finished; done; completed; dead; deceased

**pilikia**— n. *pee-lee-KEE-uh*; trouble

**pupule**— adj. *poo-POO-lay*; crazy

**wahine**— n. *wah-HEE-nay*; female; woman; women

**wiki-wiki**— adv. *WEE-kee-WEE-kee*; quickly

# ACKNOWLEDGMENTS

I could not have written this book were it not for Nancy Drew. As a child, I devoured every volume of the girl-turned-sleuth's adventures with her friends, Bess and George. I did well in school because of her by finishing all my classwork correctly in order to earn free-reading time. Then, I would lose myself in Nancy Land. My earliest allowance money was spent purchasing Nancy's entire set of mysteries. I still have all those precious books, saved for my little granddaughter. Such activities fostered in me an enduring love of mysteries, reading, and writing.

Not surprisingly, I grew up to become a teacher. So, to my former students in grades K–12 spanning my thirty-five-year career in the San Diego Unified School District, I offer my gratitude and amazement. Each of you was unique, but collectively, you shared your capacity daily to energize my abiding love of reading and writing, which brought this book to life.

Thank you, former student beta readers: Annaliese, Diana, Margot, and Michael. Thanks also to supportive friends and family: Anne, Barb, Betty, Brian, Carolyn, Colin 1, Colin 2, Connie, Deb, Erin, Janet, Jen, Kimme, Mary 1, Mary 2, Nicole, Ola, Pat, Paul 1, Paul 2, Sharon, and Virginia.

I must salute the late San Diego author Jean Ferris, who graciously read my earliest manuscript. She introduced me to her editor Deborah Halverson, who worked her magic on my text.

A special thanks to the staff at Acorn Publishing for giving my book a chance: authors and co-owners Jessica Therrien and Holly Kammier; and, the talented Lacey Impellizeri for assembling my monthly newsletter and providing other marketing tools. Editor Molly Lewis polished my work. Debra Cranfield Kennedy beautifully formatted my book for publication. Graphic artist Hayley Lekven drew the incredible map of Botanic Hill. Cover designer Dane Lowe at eBook Launch was patient with me to produce my book's gorgeous cover. I am indebted to author and friend Robin "R. D." Kardon, who referred me to Acorn Publishing, provided much support, and praised my book. Also to the talented, generous authors Lois Letchford, K. A. Fox, Sam Ashkenas, and Pamela McCord for their praise. Thank you all.

To associate professor Bryan Fry, Ph.D., Australia Research Council Fellow and head of the Venom Evolution Laboratory, School of Biological Sciences, University of Queensland, St. Lucia, Queensland, Australia, many thanks for your fascinating research and enthusiastic assistance with facts about Komodo dragons and snake venoms.

To the team at the informative website synesthesiaworld.com and the BBC documentary *Derek Tastes of Earwax,* many thanks for enlightening me about lexical-gustatory synesthesia, the rare mental ability I share with my character, Rani Kumar.

Speaking of Rani, Lanny asked her early in the mystery if anyone ever solved any crimes using synesthesia. Yes—in fiction, at least. Try Googling "synesthesia in fiction" to see how using the ability—for good and evil—has been interestingly treated in television and literature.

Last but never least, to you, my dear Readers. I hope you enjoyed the journey with our four brilliant detectives, Lexi, Lanny, Rani, and Moki, as all of you prowled the Botanic Hill environs in search of clues that solved the mystery of *Nutmeg Street: Egyptian Secrets*. Well done!

Sherrill Joseph
San Diego, California

# ABOUT THE AUTHOR

*Laurens Antoine Photography*

Sherrill Joseph's debut novel, *Nutmeg Street: Egyptian Secrets*, had been inside her head for decades. The mystery genre took hold of her as a fifth grader when she discovered Nancy Drew and Phyllis A. Whitney mysteries. Years later, it still hasn't let go.

Graduating Phi Beta Kappa and *summa cum laude* with a bachelor's degree in English literature and a master's in education, Sherrill spent the next thirty-five years as a K–12 literacy teacher. When she retired from teaching in 2013, the Botanic Hill detectives and their mysteries finally sprang to life.

Forever inspired by her beautiful students in the San Diego public schools, the author has peopled and themed the Botanic Hill Detectives Mysteries with children of various abilities, cultures, and interests. She strongly believes that embracing diversity is the key to a better world.

Sherrill is a native San Diegan where she lives in a ninety-one-year-old house in a historic neighborhood with her bichon frisé-poodle mix, Jimmy Lambchop. In addition to her dog, the city of San Diego, and reading and writing, the author loves her daughter, son-in-law, and granddaughter. She cannot omit her other passions, namely, dark chocolate, popcorn, old movies, staircases, and daisies. She is a member of SCBWI, IWSG, and the Authors' Guild and promises more adventures with the squad to come.

FOLLOW SHERRILL AT
## SHERRILLJOSEPH.COM    @MYSTERYAUTHOR7

Made in the USA
Monee, IL
02 July 2021